The Average Amish Woman

Meghan Mason

Published by Trellis Publishing, 2021.

THE AVERAGE AMISH WOMAN

First edition. July 14, 2021.

Copyright © 2021 Meghan Mason.

ISBN: 979-8224057030

Written by Meghan Mason.

THE AVERAGE AMISH WOMAN

MEGHAN MASON

Faith came through the labor of her first child a little worse for wear. It had been twenty-three agonizingly long hours of pain and worry. The good part was that she and her husband, Luke, were now blessed with a new boppli boy. After the birthing process, Faith had been far too exhausted to even hold the poor little boppli, let alone choose a name for him. Luke tried as best he could to manage the boppli alone. The midwife had mentioned that a case of the baby blues was a normal happenstance of childbirth, what with all the tumultuous hormones and all, but Luke was quickly feeling overwhelmed with trying to care for an infant, plus keep an eye on Faith as she tried to recover. It was getting a bit too much to manage. Luckily, Faith had a cousin, Sadie, who was a little older than the average Amish woman, and was available to help as a nurse to the child and to Faith, so Luke felt that now was the perfect time to broach the topic with Faith,

"Dearest, I know you have not been feeling yourself these past weeks, and I think it would be wise to ask for some help with the boppli?"

Faith, being still moody after the birth, turned her head, tears streaming down her face, as his words had unintentionally reinforced her own sense of inadequacy,

"Sure, Luke, if that's what you think is best," she cried. Luke felt terrible over causing more tears, but this was just the situation that was continuing to be a challenge,

"Oh no, Faith! No tears! You are doing just wonderful. Maddie, the midwife, said that this was a perfectly normal reaction to the hormonal fluctuations in your body. Many women go through this after the birth of a boppli. Do not feel badly over it for a second. I was thinking it would be a nice change if we asked your sweet cousin, Sadie, to help with the household chores. You can oversee boppli, and designate any other chores to Sadie," he answered, trying his best to make it sound as positive as possible. He watched closely as Faith rolled back towards him, trying her best to force a smile,

"Ok, my dear Luke. I understand it has been hard for you to handle everything on your own. Let's write to Sadie at once, then," and Luke handed her paper and pencil.

Faith had written Sadie a letter, trying not to sound overly desperate, but Sadie could tell that the new father was ready to return to the fields, and she could sense that her cousin was feeling a little depressed. Sadie had heard tale of women feeling moody after the birth of a child, although she could scarcely understand why. It was her dream to have a child, but as the time flew by, her chances of marrying and becoming a mother grew slimmer by the minute. This was of no consequence, as she knew how much Faith needed her. She put aside all other responsibilities to care for Faith and the boppli. There was not a job in the world that sounded more exciting to her in that moment than caring for her cousin and little one.

She currently lived on the outskirts of Wilkes County, so the letter had arrived with some speed. This proved lucky for Luke, who was at the end of his rope, having been dealing with soiled diapers, helping with all the laundry, and trying his best to serve as family cook. That turned out to be somewhat of a disaster, since all he did was either burn everything or serve it all miserably undercooked. He was all for being a new parent, but Amish men belonged in the fields, doing manual work for the family, whereas a woman's place was homemaking and child rearing. He hoped his wife would feel better soon, so that their lives could return to normal. Little did Luke understand that with a new boppli, there was never to be the same sense of normalcy.

Sadie had received the letter with an open and willing heart, as she had nothing much else to keep her busy nowadays. She was now well past the marriageable age of most Amish girls, being thirty already, and having had no offers of marriage, nor any suitors over the years. It had been a hard pill to swallow, being the only girl to be passed over in the entirety of Wilkes County. She had not been an unattractive young girl, but she was plainer than the rest of the girls her age. This had led to many lonely evenings at home with her parents, and since her teens and early twenties, all her bruders and schwesters had gotten married and left home. She had been left to care for her parents, but they had started their family very young, and were not nearly so old as would need constant care from their daughter.

Sadie recognized the opportunity to help her cousin, Faith, for what it was. It would be a life of servitude, although not forced, because she loved Faith, and she loved taking care of wee bopplis too. However, it was still a lonely life once the family no longer needed her help. Perhaps Faith would keep her on as a helper if she had additional bopplis. That is what Sadie wished for at the very least. Plus, Luke was a nice and upright man, who treated Faith with more respect than she had ever witnessed. Most Amish men were quite honorable, but Sadie had seen a few friends and one schwester end up with a domineering husband. Lucky Faith had been blessed two-fold with a proper husband and a beautiful little boppli. She considered the whole plan sheer providence, and packed her bags with delight, thinking of all the good times ahead with her cousin's family.

By the next morning, Sadie was safely in her father's buggy headed towards the other end of the county. There was so much to think about, as she gazed at the lovely fall foliage. October was her favorite time of year,

"Oh, daed, look at all the changing leaves!" she cried, "they are so many rich colors of gold, orange, yellow, and just a few green leaves still peeking through. By November, there'll be almost no leaves at all. Snowfall brings its own magical beauty, but I prefer the change between summer and fall. It's like a kaleidoscope of color!"

Her daed glanced up at the trees as he held the reigns,

"True," he declared, "there is no prettier time of year than fall, in my humble opinion, Sadie. But more important than the changing leaves is your new job of helping your cousin Faith. She's going to be needing lots of tender loving care, as your mamm put it to me last evening." Sadie understood what he was hinting at, since Gracie, her eldest schwester had given birth six months ago now, "When Gracie had baby Fern, she struggled with the moods for some many weeks."

"I know, and remember it well, daed," answered Sadie. "In fact, I consider it a good thing that I had a trial run of it with Gracie. Now I'll know what to expect with Faith. I do feel sorry for her, this being her first boppli and all. She should be enjoying this special time instead of feeling out of sorts. Funny how some women get moody and others don't..." and she trailed off as the gorgeous surroundings of the woods captivated her imagination. She imagined a walk through the fallen leaves, running, and then jumping into a nice big pile of leaves. Then again, she was much too old for that frivolity now. She was a grown-up woman, but without the glory of having her own family, she thought sadly. How thrilling it would be to play with her own children and her true love amongst the golden fall beauty.

Time passed rather quickly, and it was not long before Sadie and her daed pulled up the drive to Luke and Faith's farm. Luke was just coming out the front door with a basket to fetch eggs when they arrived,

"Well! If it isn't cousin Sadie and Uncle Fredrick! Welcome, and come right in," and he helped Uncle Fredrick tether the horses. Sadie grabbed her two small bags, and in they went to have tea and cake with Luke, Faith, and the new boppli,

"Isn't he just the cutest ever?" squealed Sadie, and she gathered up the boy and snuggled him, smelling the top of his little newborn head. There was nothing like the scent of a newborn, she thought, as she tucked the little one back in his cradle.

She glanced around the kitchen for Faith, but found no one there except an apron covered in flour and egg shells. Then she noticed poor Luke's plaid shirt, all dirty with the fixings of making a carrot cake! Faith must be worse off than Gracie had been. At least Grace had been able to move about the house, and do minimal choring. It looked as though Luke was primarily on his own with everything around the house and baby too! She was going to have her hands full with running around the house, plus looking after baby and mother too,

"Luke, if I may be so bold as to inquire, how is cousin Faith coping?"

"Ah, no good, I'm afraid," he said, "she goes from feeling alright to weeping for no apparent reason."

"Well, have you had the doctor in for a look at her?" she asked.

"Yep, Doc Spencer says she'll be right as rain come a few more weeks, but it's been hard taking care of boppli. He doesn't even have a name yet! Every time I ask Faith what we should call him, she starts to crying. I don't know what I'm doing wrong," Luke said with exasperation.

"I'll see what might be bothering her, but somethings just take a little healing time, Luke. It's nothing to worry yourself over unless it gets out of hand. I'm here now, and all will be well soon enough. Tomorrow morning you can start about your outside choring, and I'll do my part inside with Faith and this little one, "and she gestured towards the cooing boppli in the cradle. Luke seemed glad to hear all of this, and headed off to bed early that night to get plenty of much needed rest. As for Faith, Sadie prepared her a bowl of stew she had prepared once daed had gone, and made up a cheery tray. There was a bowl of hearty beef stew, cornbread, and a glass of milk. Sadie dropped one of the last flowers of the season into a bud vase, and carried it into Faith,

"Hello, cousin. How are you feeling?"

"I'm not too well, Sadie," she said slightly above a whisper. "I don't want to burden Luke anymore with these blues I've been feeling, and I'm afraid I haven't been very much help."

"Never you mind that right now," said Sadie, and she urged her cousin to eat.

After the bowl was clean, and the cornbread left only half eaten, Sadie figured she'd better ask Faith about what she wanted to call the boppli. He could not be nameless any longer, and that was the first hurdle topping her list of challenges.

"Faith, now Luke has been fretting over what to call the boppli. Do you have a favorite name in mind?" She could see Faith's face darken a bit, but she confided in Sadie instead of her usual crying spell, which as actually a positive step in the right direction.

"Sadie, was Gracie this way too?" she wondered. "I feel so all alone, and there are no other women in the village that have gone through these baby blues."

"Yes, it's strictly temporary, but we've got work to do if you want to be up and around in the next few months. Lying here day after day isn't doing you any favors. That's how we got Gracie to snap out of it. Now, let's start with naming boppli."

"Alright, if you say so," and she looked sincerely relieved to hear this news coming from a woman instead of Doc Spencer. It was easy to talk to Sadie. They had always been so close as young girls, but since she had married Luke, her girlhood relationships had taken a backseat to her husband and their growing family. "How about Isaac? That was Luke's daed's name, so I think that would make Luke feel happy."

"Sounds like an excellent choice to me!" exclaimed Sadie, and the two shared a few giggles, and played with Isaac, which was a vast improvement for her cousin. The next month proceeded much the same way, and it was not long before Sadie's infectious kind ways and loving heart were becoming a part of the new household.

Faith eventually found her way back to normalcy, thanks to Sadie's constant support and Luke's unwavering love. By two months, Faith was fully capable of caring for Isaac full time. She still needed some assistance with chores, so it was agreed that Sadie would stay on for an indefinite amount of time. Sadie loved the idea, because she had the joy of proximity to Isaac, and Faith and Luke were quickly becoming an important part of her life. She cooked excellently, and her meals were even becoming sort of legendary within the small village. It was a perfect fit for all concerned.

Just a few days later, Faith returned from a walk to town with baby Isaac in the pram. They had gone to mail a few letters, and she had returned to the farm brimming with news of everything that was happening in town,

"Sadie! I'm home," and she searched out her cousin in the chicken coop gathering fresh eggs and tending to the new chicks. "You'll never guess what's been going on! Old farmer Gregor finally passed away, which of course is sad news, but the exciting part is that his nephew Abraham has reportedly inherited his land. He's due to arrive in two weeks, and a committee of ladies is being formed as a welcome group. I volunteered you! You're to be his cook and housekeeper for the first month of his stay. By then he'll be sure t find a wife, and you can return to life here with us," and Faith and Sadie walked back to the kitchen to feed Isaac his afternoon snack.

"I wish you would have consulted me first, Faith. It's not a problem for me to do this service for Abraham, but I am sure a younger lady would have been much more appropriate if he is looking for a wife. He must be nervous coming to a new county and inheriting a new farm. I'll hardly be very thrilling company for the poor man," lamented Sadie.

"Nonsense!" cried her cousin, for Faith knew that Abraham was a bit older than the average young farmer, and Sadie was still pretty, even though she qualified as an old maid at thirty years old. Faith believed that this would be an advantageous situation, given that it was rumored that Abraham was not handy in the kitchen, and needed a housekeeper too. These were natural talents that Sadie had been blessed with, and she was caring too, which would serve him well being new in a strange village. At the very least, Sadie would make a new friend, and Faith would have a little more room to get used to doing more household chores.

Late that following Friday afternoon, Abraham ambled into town on his horse, carrying what little belongings he had in his buggy. The committee was there to welcome him to Wilkes County, and introduce him to various members of the town. Faith and Luke, being pillars of faith in their community, explained to Abraham all he needed to know about worship, work, and social life. They explained to him that there was to be a social after worship in two weeks' time, and that everyone looked forward to meeting him. He got settled at Old Farmer Gregor's property, and Sadie was sent to prepare dinner and keep house. She was to make the moderately long walk from Luke and Faith's farm to the next farm, which was now Abraham's.

As Sadie stood at the counter slicing vegetables, Abraham engaged her in conversation,

"So, Sadie, is it?"

"Yes, my name is Sadie. What can I do for you? I'm in the middle of cooking your supper, so it'll have to be quick," she replied, trying not to sound annoyed that her cooking was being disturbed.

"Oh, in that case, I'll wait to talk. It smells heavenly, whatever it is," answered a confident Abraham.

He was a handsome man, sure to be a big hit with the young ladies who were vying for a husband, she thought, and she continued to prepare the roasted chicken with care. She wanted to please him as a cook, so that she might stay at this post for as long as possible. She had grown used to the community, and did not relish the dismal thought of returning to her parents on the other end of the county. There was absolutely nothing waiting for her there, and at least here, people appreciated her for what she could offer; excellent cooking, strong faith, and limitless kindness for others. This was not going unnoticed by Abraham, to which Sadie was oblivious. He was about thirty she guessed, but it was usual for a man like him to take a young wife, and be ready to start a family and tend to a farm or similar livelihood.

When the chicken was roasted to perfection, and the vegetables and potatoes were finished boiling, she laid out a place for him at his table. She called him to supper time, but once he saw only the one place setting, he insisted that she join him,

"Heavens, no! There is so much great food here for only me. Surely you can sit and join me. If I may now regale you with some light conversation," he joked, since she had put him in his place earlier. Though unorthodox for the two to sit together, she agreed. He seemed congenial and honest, and she was truthfully quite hungry,

"So, tell me, Sadie, what brings you here to my farmhouse to help with choring?"

"I have been elected to serve as your housekeeper and cook until you find a proper replacement," she replied matter-of-factly.

"Oh, you mean until I am suitable married to one of the eligible young ladies?" he smiled.

"Well, yes, that's the way things normally go. You know that," and she did not appreciate him playing as though he did not understand what was expected of them all.

"And, you, Sadie, what is expected of you?"

"Nothing," she stopped short, and did not know exactly how to reply to this, as she was never asked before.

"May I ask why you are not amongst the clamoring ladies looking for a husband?"

She shied away, and stared at the floor, not knowing if he meant to be insulting or what his purpose was. He had to know that at her age she was considered a spinster, though relatively the same age as he was. That was tradition, and as Amish, they all knew full well what was expected. She continued to look away, feeling ashamed and saddened that she had not been chosen to be a wife and mother. It was enough to bear the brunt of the feeling of failure every day, but she was wholly unused to being confronted with the obvious truth of her situation.

Abraham seemed to notice her discomfort, and immediately regretted his comment,

"Please, Sadie, I apologize if I have made you feel less than what you deserve," and at that she looked up in some surprise. What she *deserved*? Wasn't this what she deserved? She was bound to a life of serving others through faith, perseverance, and volunteering in the community to help those in need. That was what she thought she deserved, and nothing more. She had resigned herself to her fate, and did not appreciate the fact thrown in her face. She felt embarrassed and self-conscious, but stood up for herself nonetheless,

"I beg your pardon, Bruder Abraham, but I am too old for marriage, and you, being an Amish man should know this. I have been elected to serve you because I am not what one would consider eligible, and no one need fear for my reputation at my age."

"That, Sadie is one of the most stupid things I have ever heard, and yes, I know full well what is traditional for Amish, but that does not mean I have to agree with it. What is wrong with you? Nothing! You and I are probably the same age, and you are attractive," at which she blushed furiously. No matter how hard she tried, she felt the heat in her cheeks increase, although she felt a twinge of instant attraction for a man who spoke his mind, and who also thought her pretty. What would she say to a man such as this, she pondered, but she blurted out what came into her head,

"Why! Bruder Abraham, while I thank you for the compliment, I think it better that you concentrate on your chicken. There is blackberry pie for dessert, but none for you should your dinner be left unfinished," and they sat in relative silence for the remainder of the meal, though Abraham felt vindicated with the offer of freshly baked pie!

Their banter continued as such during every meal, becoming more and more relaxed with one another, though Sadie knew her place. She was perhaps a friend, and nothing more. She would not fool herself into believing anything more. Besides, Bruder Abraham had been away for three out of five dinners this week alone. Parents were inviting him to meet daughters, and he was being plied with all the best traditional foods the women of the house could manage. As if a streusel would entice a man to marry, she clucked, as she finished the dishes from the day, and prepared to sit down with a nice, hot cup of mint tea. She was determined to enjoy her times alone, and either read a book or sit with a cup of tea until Abraham arrived back for his late night habitual coffee. She did not understand the man's need for coffee that late at night, but her job was not to question why, but only to fulfil her duties to the man. She was growing fond of spending time with him, and even enjoyed their lively conversations about social conventions and everyday talk of farming, food, and faith. They never ran out of topics to speak about, and he insisted she join him for every meal.

Just as she retired to the couch for her tea, she heard Abraham and his buggy in the yard. Home early tonight, she thought, and went to put the kettle back on the stove for coffee, "And why are you home so early this night?" she inquired.

"Ah, no reason besides a little boredom," and he hung his hat on the stand, and plopped down on a chair, "Would there be any corn fritters left over from last evening?"

"Why would you want fritters when you just came from supper at the Smith farm?"

"Because the women are apparently not very good at cooking! They may have beautiful and upright daughters, but your corn fritters are by far the best in all the county, Sadie," he said with a hint of a smile, though he looked exhausted of going out almost every night to meet new families and their daughters. Sadie had a few fritters left, and warmed them at the stove. She served them with his coffee, and sat down to her tea across the room.

Abraham devoured a fritter and a gulp of coffee, and then launched into conversation,

"Sadie, enough is enough. You know we get along well, and I have already said that I find you attractive. Why must I continue going to these ridiculous suppers, when I know what I want out of life already?" Sadie rocked in her rocking chair, completely oblivious to what was about to be said between them. She felt they were friends and good ones at that, but nothing more.

"Sadie, are you listening to me?" he said, as she stared off into her book, "I am trying to speak with you, and you've got your head stuck in a book?"

"I apologize, Abraham, what on earth do you want to talk about? Aren't you too tired for anymore frivolous conversation after all these suppers?"

"That's exactly the point. Why should I go elsewhere when I am happy here at home?" he asked, as she just sat there, mouth agape, and provided the expected answer,

"You will not be allowed your bachelorhood for very much longer. You may as well choose one of the many pretty girls, and put an end to this coming and going..." she sighed. She knew in her deepest heart of hearts that she loved Abraham, but that destiny was not hers, and she had accepted that fact very early on. She looked up from her bible readings, and found Abraham looking at her differently than most nights,

"I am done with the suppers. You are right, Sadie. They will never give up until I have chosen a wife. In fact, that is one reason why I am home early tonight, besides the terrible cooking," he jested. She put her tea down upon the table, and she felt the sadness she expected to feel once he had made the inevitable choice. No matter her own feelings, she knew what was coming next. He had found one of the Smith girls acceptable, and this was what he was trying to tell her, that he would not much longer be in need of a housekeeper or a cook. Abraham continued to look at her, so she figured she'd better say some congratulatory words, even if she feared her displacement was imminent. Not only would she lose her new friend, but she would have to return to her parents in the east of the county,

"What can I say, Abraham? This is wonderful news that you have chosen a wife for yourself. I will miss keeping house for you, but now you must make room for a wife. No doubt there will be many preparations to be made for a wedding," and she went back to reading her verses.

"Yes, no doubt about all that fuss, though I am a simple man. And, yes, I have decided on a wife. But I hope you'll stay on to cook and clean for me after I am married," he said straight faced.

"You of all people know that is impossible. If you didn't enjoy her cooking, you had better choose someone else then. No wife is going to want an old maid hanging around the house," she countered.

"No, I don't suppose she would, but sometimes old maids make the best wives," he said, "so in theory, I would not have to let you go, nor would I have to choose a better cook." He looked at her expectantly, though he knew well enough that he was treading on thin ice with her. He thought for certain that they would make the perfect pair, despite the unwanted gossip from the townspeople.

"I do not appreciate your jokes, Abraham. Make a choice, and do not mock those of us who have a different calling in life. Being an 'old maid' as you so nicely put it, has its advantages," though she couldn't really think of a good example just then.

"Woman, are you really that dense that you do not understand my meaning? I am saying in the best way possible that I prefer my wife to be the old maid that I already love!" She looked at him utterly astounded. If this was not the cruelest joke ever played, she did not know what could be worse. However, Abraham looked at her sincerely, and looked expectantly for some sort of answer, so she replied,

"Ha ha, Abraham. You've had your little joke at my expense. Now off to bed with you, and after that stunt you can bet there won't be any more extra fritters!"

"No, no, dear Sadie! I am saying quite deliberately that you are the wife I have chosen if you will have me as your husband. We make a good match, you and me. We are the same age, we love the same things, and we are excellent friends. Why not that I should choose you? You are the best choice for me, and that is the way I want our lives to be. Not this stiff situation of living as acquaintances, when we both know we are suited well for one another. Please say yes, Sadie, or make me a miserable old Amish man who never marries or has any offspring!" he declared with so much vigor that Sadie had little other choice but to believe him.

"What? Me? I am just that, an old maid. Besides, I may not be able to bear children…" and he stopped her there,

"That's nonsense. Women your age bear children all the time. The only difference is that they are already married by this time. Stop devaluing yourself! I love you, Sadie, and you're not going anywhere unless you say you do not love me too. Now what do you say to that?"

She stood now, tea cup clattered to the floor, open-mouthed in total surprise, but she already knew what her answer was to be,

"Yes, I do love you," she blushed, "and I do want to marry you too, but you will set the tongues a-wagging by choosing me over the younger ones!"

"I do not care about wagging tongues. I care about keeping the woman I love in my home, and making her my wife."

"Then yes! I do accept." She bent down to pick up the pieces of shattered cup, but Abraham beat her to it, and began to gather the pieces. "I guess we will need a new set of cups for our first wedding gift," he said seriously, but the humor was not lost on Sadie. She let out a giggle, sounding more like a school girl than a grown woman of thirty. Her parents and Faith and Luke would never believe this turn of events in a million years, though she was utterly happy to accept the proposal. Not only was she to be married, she was to marry a man who she felt real friendship for, and sometimes that was a rarity in marriages.

Four Months Later

The wedding was very simple, and her parents came in the buggy, and Faith, Luke and Isaac were the only guests in attendance. Not by circumstance, but by choice. The simpler the better, they both thought, and they had already sent the town into a flurry of confusion as to why Abraham would choose a spinster as a wife, but he had quickly put them all in their places, quoting Jeremiah, 29:11,

"For I know the plans I have for you," declares the LORD, "plans to prosper you and not to harm you, plans to give you hope and a future."

Once Abraham's words had been passed around town, there was no one who could argue otherwise that the marriage should take place. So, a hasty date was set, allowing for travel time for Sadie's thrilled parents. They initially did not know quite what to make of the situation, but after meeting Abraham, they were relieved to know that he was an upstanding Amish man, who loved their daughter very much. Her daed even lamented losing a great cook to Abraham, to which her mamm had good naturedly bristled, but all knew that Abraham was to become a very fortunate man.

Eighteen short months later, Faith announced a second pregnancy, but the true celebration was about to begin, as Sadie confided in her cousin that she too was expecting a child. It was more than she could have ever dreamt of! God had blessed them all beyond measure, and now the cousins would be having their bopplis very close together. The second cousins would grow up being the best of friends!

9 months Later

Sadie had felt that nine months was hardly enough time to prepare for the arrival of a new boppli, and she had worked tirelessly knitting and crocheting baby things. She and Faith even joined a quilting circle and made two new little quilts for the upcoming new additions. They both chose yellow and green fabrics, not knowing ahead of time whether they would be blessed with boys or girls. Sadie secretly wished for a baby girl, so that she could make her lots of dollies and play clothes, while Faith had been hoping for another little boy. Luke prided himself on his son, and was praying for a big group of bruders for little Isaac, but Faith had put her foot down at having two. Luke was to be happy with whatever he got, and he loved to joke relentlessly that Faith would be a new mother again and again, delivering son after son to a proud and overjoyed father. Whatever the case was to be, Luke reminded Faith what a time they had had with baby Isaac, and that a healthy, bouncing boppli was all that he truly cared about.

Labor pains began for the two women almost a day apart, and a brand new, precious boppli girl was born to Abraham and Sadie, and they named her Esther, because Abraham had had a spinster aunt that had died childless and alone. Esther was a tribute to her, and to the blessing that had been bestowed upon them. However, before Doc Spencer and the midwife could gather their things, it was obvious that Sadie was still in distress of labor pains. The only conclusion to be made, was that another sweet boppli was about to make an appearance!

"Twins!" Abraham exclaimed upon hearing the news from the birthing room. He was overjoyed, though Sadie was shocked to say the least. Here she had thought it would be difficult to have just one boppli, but here they were with two. So, Esther had a sister, and her name was to be Ella. Ella had long been a favorite name of Sadie's since her childhood, so it was only fitting that one parent named one daughter, and the other named the second little dear one. Esther and Ella would be the happiest set of sisters the village had ever seen.

As for Faith and Luke, they had another boy, and called him Abram, not to be confused with Abraham!

Sadie's mamm and daed decided to move closer, so her mamm could help with all three bopplis. And so it was that the blessing was four-fold, three new bopplis, and grandparents close to boot. God had been good to all of them, and much joy was to be had by all involved. Even the townsfolk did their best to help with the extra work of three bopplis in two families.

Abraham had never been prouder of any decision that he had ever made before in his life. Marrying Sadie had been the best thing ever, and now their little family was complete.

Little did Abraham and Sadie realize then, that two more bopplis would make an appearance in the coming years. Their happy family of three would turn into a family of five, with two little bruders for the girls. They were born one year apart, and Sadie's heart was filled to brimming with gifts she never thought would be hers.

ABIGAIL'S DILEMMA
SAMANTHA COLLIER

Abigail Esh watched as the familiar hills and plains of her small Pennsylvania community fell into view. It had been a long buggy ride; they had been travelling for half a day.

She felt a small stab of excitement, at the thought of finally coming home. She had been staying with some friends of her family, who were English, for the past month. It was all part of her *rumspringa*. She had sampled many things in the big city, including going to art galleries and English restaurants. It had been enjoyable, of course, and she wouldn't change the experience for the world.

But she wanted to return to her community, and start life as a fully committed adult Amish. She was ready.

At last. Her family's farmhouse was in view.

As the buggy pulled up, her eyes took in every detail: the old ramshackle farmhouse, the outbuildings and hen house. Home.

The front door opened, and her mother was down the veranda steps. Her eyes were shining in excitement.

"Abigail! We thought you'd never get here," she remarked.

Abigail stepped down from the buggy, embracing her mother. It felt like she hadn't seen her in years.

"Mammi! It is so good to be home," she said. "Where is everybody?"

Mrs Esh smiled, a bit indulgently. "Daughter of mine, have you forgotten the routine already?" They walked up the steps to the house, arm in arm. "Your father and brothers are in the fields, of course. They will return for lunch, as is always the way. Your sisters are quilting, over at Mrs Troyer's, as they do every Tuesday."

Abigail flung herself onto the living room sofa as soon as they entered. "It was such a long trip, Mammi. I feel black and blue all over."

"How are the Carlisles?" Mrs Esh walked to the kitchen as she spoke, getting the coffee she had just made and two cups.

"Very good." Abigail sat up, rubbing her eyes. "They send their best wishes. It was a bit of a whirlwind, staying with them."

"I could imagine." Mrs Esh poured the coffee. "Come, have your coffee. It will revitalise you."

Abigail did as her mother requested, walking to the table.

Suddenly, she stopped. She could see the figure of a man at the front door – tall, dressed in the traditional Amish clothing. He had taken his hat off.

Who was he? She had never seen him before. And her eyes seemed to be unaccustomed to the Amish dress. She had been so used to seeing English clothes that it stood out to her. Well, she would get used to it, again, of course.

"Mammi." Abigail gestured toward the door. "Someone is here."

Mrs Esh rose, approaching the door. "Oh, it is only Nicholas! He is helping your father and brothers; he has been here about two weeks, from another county." She opened the door. "Nicholas! What can I do for you?"

The young man smiled shyly, looking from Mrs Esh to Abigail. "I am sorry to disturb you, Mrs Esh. Your husband sent me to tell you not to prepare lunch today, as we are planning to work through."

"Work through?" Mrs Esh frowned. "Stay for a moment, Nicholas. I will prepare something quickly for you all to eat, which you can take back with you. You can't all work from dawn to sundown without food in your bellies. Please, come in and sit down while I get something ready."

Nicholas hesitated, then walked through the door.

"Abigail," Mrs Esh said, "Could you please pour Nicholas a coffee, while I get the food ready."

"Of course, Mammi," said Abigail, glancing sideways at the handsome, shy young man. Who was he? Why was he working here?

"I'm Abigail," she said. "Please, sit down."

The young man did as he was told. Abigail poured him a coffee, then sat down beside him.

"How did you come to work with us?" she asked, taking a sip of her own drink.

"I was looking for some short term work," Nicholas replied, blushing slightly. "I am on my *rumspringa*, and wanted to experience life outside my community for a bit. My father knows yours, from many years ago, and got in contact." He paused, staring at her. "I'm sorry, but you are Abigail, who has been on your own *rumspringa*?"

"*Ja*," Abigail agreed. "I have only just returned, after staying with some English friends in the city."

"Did you have a good time?"

"I did," Abigail said. She looked at his hands gripping the coffee cup. Strong, and firm. "But I am happy to be home. The city life is not for me. The Lord has made that very clear."

"I am glad," he said, smiling at her. He had the bluest of eyes, the colour of the sky on a bright summer's day.

Mrs Esh came back in, carrying a paper bag filled with sandwiches. She handed it to Nicholas.

"Please, finish your coffee," she said, as he stood up.

"Thank you Mrs Esh, but I must return to work," he said. "And thank you for the food. I am sure we will all appreciate it."

He smiled at Abigail, ducking his head. Then he left.

Abigail stared after him, sipping her coffee thoughtfully.

What a handsome young man. And such polite manners.

It was good to be home, for a lot of reasons. And it seemed that there was one more good reason, although Abigail hadn't realised when she had walked through the door.

The day was full of surprises.

***

Now that she was home, it seemed like she had never left. It was funny, how life worked in that way.

She had already been home a week, and was back into the old routine. And the most exciting thing of all was that Nicholas, the shy young man who was helping her family with the harvest, had asked her out on a date.

She didn't know where they were going, as she excitedly got herself ready on Saturday night. But she knew that Nicholas would take her somewhere appropriate, as well as fun. They had just clicked, right from the moment that she had laid eyes on him at the front door.

But he was shy. She had found many reasons to go and disturb her family as they worked, sometimes bringing snacks or drinks. Her brothers would grin at her – they knew what she was up to. She didn't usually come to visit them so often. It had worked. Eventually, Nicholas had asked her out.

Now they sat in Stoll's restaurant in town, having just finished a hearty meal and laughing over a coffee.

Abigail had never been able to speak so easily to a boy. It was like they couldn't keep up with everything they wanted to say to each other. She felt a glow within her, as she looked at him.

They were just thinking of leaving when the door to the restaurant opened. Abigail turned to look automatically. Then wished she hadn't.

Oh, no. It was Christian Raber. She swivelled quickly in her seat, staring straight ahead. Her heart had started to thump uncomfortably. Maybe, if she was lucky, he hadn't seen her.

But her luck wasn't in. She heard his footsteps behind, approaching their table.

"Abigail." He wasn't smiling. "I didn't know that you were back in town."

She turned and looked at him, a bit fearfully. "Just a week," she said, quickly.

Nicholas was looking from Abigail to Christian. He seemed perplexed.

"I am Christian Raber," the man said, extending a hand toward Nicholas. "Abigail has lost her manners, it seems."

Nicholas took the man's hand, shaking it. He looked at Abigail. "And I am Nicholas Fisher."

She stood up, quickly. "We were just leaving, Christian," she said, walking toward the door. Nicholas' eyes widened, but he stood up, too, almost forgetting his hat on the table as he followed her. He had to go back to get it.

They exited, into the cold night.

Christian stood for a moment, staring after them.

His eyes were cold.

***

"What was that all about?" Nicholas had to run to catch up to Abigail.

She turned, stopping to catch her breath. "I'm sorry," she said. "I know that I appeared rude. But I didn't want to speak to him. He has this idea that he is in love with me, and I have given him no encouragement. Honestly." She blinked back tears, staring up at him.

"What does he do?" Nicholas was frowning, staring down at her.

"Oh, nothing much," said Abigail. She was appalled to find that her hands were shaking. Stop it, she told herself. "He is always polite. He just doesn't seem to understand that I am not interested."

She paused, shaking her head slightly. "I have told him enough times. But he doesn't seem to understand. When I next see him, at Church or Evening Sing or wherever, he asks me out again, as if he hasn't listened at all."

Nicholas assisted her up into the buggy. "I am sorry, Abigail. It is hard when someone doesn't listen to you."

"*Ja*," she agreed. She tried to shake the image of Christian, in the restaurant, out of her mind. She was on a date, with Nicholas. Handsome, caring Nicholas.

"Don't worry about it," she said. "I am sure he will realise, eventually."

They rode off, into the night.

They didn't look back. If they had, they might have seen the figure of Christian, standing in the dark street, staring after the buggy long after it had disappeared.

***

"He was in Stoll's Restaurant, Mamm."

Abigail was having a hot cocoa with her mother after the date. Nicholas had dropped her off half an hour ago.

Mrs Esh frowned. "Don't read anything into it, Abigail," she said. "It might have been just co-incidence. Who knows, maybe he needed to get something from Stoll's."

"At nine-thirty on a Saturday night?" Abigail was frowning, too. "No, I know him of old. He followed me there, I am sure of it."

"He never threatens you, does he?" Her mother looked at her over the brim of the mug.

"No." Abigail shook her head. "He is always polite. It's just a feeling I get. He always seems to be where I go, and he won't stop asking me to date him. I think after the first three negatives, he might get the message that I am simply not interested in him in that way. But he never does."

Mrs Esh stood up. "Time for bed, I think. I will talk to your father about this. We don't want to offend the Raber's, but Christian needs to know that he can't harass you. We will have to think it through carefully, though."

Abigail nodded, bringing her mug to the kitchen sink.

"I almost forgot." Her mother looked at her. "How was the date with Nicholas? We got so caught up talking about Christian."

Abigail smiled broadly. "It was lovely," she beamed. "I think that I really like him, Mamm. Do you think he likes me, too?"

Mrs Esh smiled, her eyes softening as she looked at her lovely daughter. "How could he not, my *lieb*?" she replied. "But I don't know how long he is staying for, Abigail. Your father said that he only needed help for a few weeks, and they are almost up. He lives in the next county."

"That's not so far," said Abigail. "We could write letters."

"So you could," agreed her mother. "But it really is time for bed now, Abigail. We have Church tomorrow, don't forget. And I have to be up very early to cook the goose for the lunch."

Abigail followed her mother up the stairs, preparing for bed. She glanced down at her Bible, thinking whether she should look at it tonight or not. It was very late. But she was still feeling jittery after her encounter with Christian, and felt like she needed some comfort.

Her head was drooping over the good book when she suddenly jolted fully awake. What had disturbed her?

She took her candle, and got out of the bed, walking to her window. She peered out into the darkness, but she could see nothing. She tried to shake the feeling of unease away from her. She was being silly. She should blow out the candle, and climb back into bed.

And yet she stayed, staring out the window. It was complete darkness; not even the moon was out tonight, and a thick blanket of clouds had covered up the stars.

She dropped the curtain, and climbed back into bed.

But the unease didn't leave her. Instead, it invaded her dreams...

She was running.

In motion, she suddenly stopped. She looked down at her feet, willing them to move. But it was like they were frozen in quicksand; the more she tried to dislodge them, the firmer they set. She twisted and turned, in a frantic bid to free herself.

He was coming. She knew he was right behind her.

Suddenly, the quicksand turned to ice. She attempted to run, again. But her feet were sliding over the ice. She stumbled, trying to regain her balance.

She heard a noise behind her, and turned quickly.

It was him. She couldn't see him in the shadows, but she knew.

The ice started cracking underneath her feet. She watched it zig-zag, broken veins across the white surface.

And then she was gone, underneath the ice, plunged into cold, cold water.

She stared up, and saw him looking down at her, coldly...

She sat up in bed, breathing heavily. She could feel sweat sliding down her neck.

This had to stop. She didn't know what Christian's intentions were, but he had to know how much he was scaring her. She didn't think that he would harm her, not really. But he was behaving oddly, and she couldn't deny anymore that it was starting to affect her.

She lay back down, drifting back to sleep. Think happy thoughts, she told herself.

The image of Nicholas filled her mind. His handsome face, concerned for her that night when she had told him about Christian. The way that he had helped her down from the buggy when they had arrived home, holding her hand tenderly so that she wouldn't slip. She had looked into his eyes, and seen kindness. His eyes shone with the purity of his soul.

Nicholas. Was she falling in love with him? But she hardly knew him. It had only been their first date, and they had chatted a handful of times before.

And soon he would leave. Return to his farm in the next county, away from her. His *rumspringa* over, just like hers was.

Would she see him again?

The image of Nicholas was the last thing that she remembered as sleep finally claimed her – this time for the whole night.

***

Abigail yawned, trying to stifle it with her hand discreetly.

It was the next day, and she was tired. It had been late before she had finally drifted off to sleep. She looked around at the familiar faces at the church service, but she hadn't seen him yet.

Nicholas. Her heart leapt as she said his name in her head, over and over.

Where could he be?

She tried to concentrate on the service, but her mind was drifting. Her mother had told her that Nicholas had attended their church service since he had been staying with them. And he himself had said that he would see her there. He had been looking forward to her mother's baked goose with apple and cider gravy for lunch, as well.

She surreptitiously scanned the congregation, again. But then she saw Christian Raber, staring at her from the back row. Shivers coursed through her; her skin crawled like it had been invaded by an army of ants.

She looked to the front, trying to concentrate on the service.

But her eyes, sickeningly, were drawn back to him.

He hadn't stopped staring. But now he added a small smile.

She refused to smile back. It would just encourage him. Silly, she chided herself. Even turning her head to look at him again he would perceive as encouragement.

He had always been an intense boy, ever since they had shared a seat in the one room classroom down the road. She could remember that he often would be alone, kicking a stone in the playground while groups around him played. And when he had friends, it would always be only one person, or two. Usually children who were a bit odd, like himself.

She had never been anything but polite to him, but she had drawn the line at friendship. She just couldn't stomach his intense stares. How he had perceived her politeness as anything other than that was beyond her. And yet he had. He had been asking her out for over six months now.

At first, she had been flattered, despite herself. But then it had got annoying. He simply wouldn't listen to her, when she said no. And then he started turning up everywhere that she went: a visit to the bakery, or when she was perusing stalls at the market. Anywhere.

It was one of the reasons she had gone so far away for *rumspringa*. Abigail wasn't much of a traveller, really. She probably would have stayed closer to home. But she had needed a break from his constant attention.

The service finally finished, and people started socialising. She went up to her mother.

"Where is Nicholas?" she whispered. "I haven't seen him today."

Mrs Esh looked at her. "I'm sorry, I forgot to tell you, Abigail," she said. "Nicholas received a note this morning, about something urgent. He needed to return home immediately. I'm not sure if he will be back, my *lieb*. He was due to finish work soon with us, anyway." She looked at her daughter. "Cheer up! You can still write to each other."

Abigail felt her heart sink. She shouldn't be so disappointed, of course. They had only had one date, and Nicholas had a life of his own, far away.

But she *was* disappointed. She couldn't deny it.

She was staring at the wall of the barn, lost in her own thoughts. She didn't see Christian approach until it was too late.

"Abigail." He bowed, slightly. His cold eyes were assessing her, as always. She often felt he looked at her like something strange he had just discovered on the sole of his shoe.

"Christian, I'm sorry, but now is not a good time," she said, quickly. Why was he always silent when he approached her? If she had some warning, she could have scurried away.

"I hear that the young man you went on a date with last night has left us," he continued, as if she hadn't spoken at all. "Very suddenly. Did you know that Frannie Glick knows him and his family? She was just telling me that he has a fiancée, back home."

Abigail gasped. She shook her head. "No, Christian, I am sure that you are mistaken," she replied. "Nicholas didn't mention anything to me about a fiancée. He is an honourable man."

"Is he?" Christian smiled, coldly. "How well do you really know him, Abigail?"

She frowned. She supposed it was true, to a degree. She had only known Nicholas a week, after all.

But she trusted her instincts. He was a good man, she knew it. He wouldn't have deliberately deceived her about having a fiancée.

"Well, I shall talk to him," she said, turning away. "I really must go, Christian. I have to help my mother with the lunch."

She walked away quickly, ducking amongst people. Hopefully he wouldn't follow her.

Was it true? He had said he had got the information from Frannie Glick. She looked around, but couldn't see her.

She frowned. Oh, well. Frannie would turn up, sooner or later. And then she would ask her, how she had come by this information that Nicholas had a fiancée.

As Christian claimed.

She felt the skin crawling on the back of her neck. She looked around, and, of course, he was staring at her. An upsurge of anger shot through her. Would he ever leave her alone?

***

"He did mention a girl he had been dating..." Mrs Esh frowned, squinting her eyes, trying to remember. "Or was it that they had dated in the past? I'm sorry, Abigail. I simply don't remember. But he never mentioned a fiancée, of that I am sure."

Abigail frowned, too. It wasn't the simple yes or no answer that she was wanting. This was very frustrating.

She didn't have a right to demand an answer of Nicholas. They had made no promises to each other; it had only been one date, after all. But she also felt that he did owe her an answer, because it simply wasn't done to be dating someone behind his fiancée's back, if he had one.

If it was true, she never would have agreed to go out with him. It was as simple as that.

Restless, Abigail stood up. "Do you need me for anything else, Mamm? If not, I might go to my room, study my bible for a while."

Mrs Esh looked at her. "Of course, Abigail," she said. "Just come down to help with supper, that's all I require."

Abigail left, bounding up the stairs.

Mrs Esh watched her go, shaking her head slightly.

Her daughter was in a state, and had been since Nicholas had left so suddenly the day before. Mrs Esh was worried about her. It was unlike Abigail. And what was this business with Christian Raber? Abigail hadn't mentioned it to her until after her date with Nicholas. If it was true, it wasn't good, and they should intervene on her behalf. But what if Abigail was just being fanciful? The Rabers were good friends of theirs. Mrs Esh didn't want to cause conflict without reason.

She frowned, pondering. No, they would do nothing, for now. If Abigail continued to be worried, well, they would do something then.

She sighed. It was hard, being young. Navigating your way into adulthood. She might mention some bible passages that Abigail should study, to try to ease her mind.

***

Abigail finished the letter, signing her name at the bottom thoughtfully.

She had been in two minds about whether to write to Nicholas, but she was so wound up she didn't know what else to do. Even if she didn't send the letter, it had felt good to get her thoughts and feelings out onto paper.

She read back over what she had written. She had tried to not be too intense, but still convey her wish to continue corresponding with him. She hadn't mentioned anything about him having a fiancée, except to implicitly imply that if he was seeing someone where he lived, she would stop communicating with him.

She put the letter in an envelope, and sealed it. She wasn't sure of his address; she would have to ask her mother if she knew it.

She left it on her desk, propped up against her lantern.

It was time to help her mother with supper.

***

Outside the farmhouse, Christian could see Abigail leave her desk. He saw the letter. He could guess who it was to. And he knew how to solve this, as well.

He often watched her. He had found a position, quite hidden. He would come over the back way to the house, through the fields, being careful to avoid her father and her brothers working.

He didn't think that he was doing anything wrong. He had, after all, explained to her that he wanted to take her out. It was his intention to make her his wife. She was hesitant, and had said no, but that didn't unduly concern him. His father had told him that girls sometimes said no when they meant yes. His own mother, apparently, had refused his father a few times before finally agreeing to date him.

She just needed a little bit of persuasion, that was all.

He frowned, thinking of when he had walked into the restaurant and seen her on a date. It simply would not do. No other man was allowed to date his Abigail.

It had been a stroke of luck that Nicholas Fisher's father had suddenly needed him back at home; as soon as he had heard that, he seized the opportunity. Frannie Glick was away on her *rumspringa*, and couldn't contradict his story about a fiancée. Frannie was a friend of his, anyway, and as soon as she was back he would contact her and persuade her to corroborate the story.

He smiled. It was all going to plan. He had to get rid of Nicholas once and for all, discredit him in Abigail's eyes. And then he would be there, to pick up the pieces.

She would finally see that he was the one for her.

***

The letter had been sent. Abigail waited for a response, but none came.

Inside, she fretted a little. It was all so strange. She had thought that she and Nicholas had a real connection. But he wasn't responding to her – did that mean that what Christian said was true? That Nicholas had a fiancée back home, and that she had been a diversion while he was away?

But as the days went by, and no letter came, Abigail had to admit it to herself. Nicholas didn't care.

Oh, well. She went about her chores as normal, and smiled and laughed when she was required to. She let no one see her sorrow. It would get better, in time. Of course, it would. They had only known each other a short time. It wasn't as if it was a deep wound.

She studied her bible. The classic passage from Ecclesiastes 3:4, about there being a time for sorrow as well as joy, comforted her. She knew that life couldn't be good, all the time. You could learn from sorrow, and had to accept that sometimes there was sorrow in life. As surely as the tides ebb and flow on the shore, sorrow and joy would come and go.

So Abigail kept telling herself, as the days drifted into weeks.

***

The women sat around the table, picking up their needles to commence their quilting bee.

Abigail picked up hers with a sigh. It had been three weeks, and she had not received a word from Nicholas. It was time to let it go, put it behind her. They had connected, but he had decided that it wasn't worth pursuing. Or, he did have a fiancée at home, and he had been merely dallying with her. Abigail preferred to think it was the former; she didn't want her last impression to be that he was a dishonourable man.

They heard another buggy pulling up outside the farmhouse. The women looked at each other.

"Are we expecting someone else?" Mrs Esh turned to the women.

Frannie Glick walked through the door, puffing slightly.

"Frannie!" Mrs Mueller put down her needle. "We weren't expecting you! Aren't you supposed to be on your *rumspringa*?"

"*Ja*," answered Frannie, smiling at the group. "I returned yesterday, a few days early. Mammi told me that you were meeting today, and I wanted to catch up with you all."

Frannie took her seat, and started answering questions about her *rumspringa*. She had been staying with cousins in Ohio, and had a wonderful time.

Abigail glanced at her as she worked. She was waiting for the break, so she could ask her about Nicholas. It probably didn't matter, anymore. But she wanted to know.

At last, the women started getting up. One went to the kitchen, to prepare coffee and snacks. Frannie rose, and walked to the window.

"Frannie," Abigail said, walking up to her. "It is nice to have you back. I was just interested to know. Christian Raber was telling me that you know Nicholas Fisher and his family."

"Who?" Frannie looked at her, a puzzled expression on her face. "I don't know any Nicholas Fisher, Abigail. I think you must be mistaken."

"Are you sure?" Abigail frowned. "Christian told me that you knew the family, and that Nicholas had a fiancée back where he lives."

Frannie continued to look at her, bewildered. "I have no idea what you are talking about, Abigail. The only Nicholas I know is Nicholas King, who we went to school with."

"I'm sorry," Abigail said. "I must have misheard him. Thank you, anyway."

She turned around, and walked out of the house. She needed to be alone, for a moment. She needed to think.

She sat down on a seat on the porch, thinking deeply.

Frannie didn't know the Fishers. She had never heard of Nicholas. Which meant one thing: Christian had lied to her. About Frannie knowing them, but also about Nicholas having a fiancée.

She felt herself go cold. This was getting serious.

Christian had always been an annoyance. But now, he was actively interfering in her life.

She didn't know what to do. Just that it had to stop, once and for all. He had no right, and she was going to make sure that he knew it.

***

Abigail dressed carefully for the meeting.

She had spoken to Mrs Raber, asking her could she come over for a visit. There was something she needed to discuss with her and her husband, urgently. She also requested that Christian be there for the meeting.

She didn't tell her mother. She knew that she would be concerned about making waves with the Rabers. It was something she was concerned about, too. But she also knew that it couldn't continue. Christian had to be stopped. And the best way of ensuring that was to enlist his parents. Abigail knew Christian. He was obedient to his parents, and his father ruled him with an iron fist.

And it was something that she felt must do, by herself. She had to stand up for herself, once and for all.

Mrs Raber opened the door, and led her to the kitchen table. Coffee and cakes were there, waiting.

"Oh, you shouldn't have gone to so much trouble," Abigail said. She was sweating, a little, and her hands when she took the coffee cup were shaking. She wasn't looking forward to this.

Mr Raber was already there, looking at her expectantly. And then Christian came into the room.

He didn't look happy. But he sat down at the table. Obviously, his parents had insisted.

"So." Mrs Raber looked at Abigail, expectantly. "What did you need to see us about so urgently, Abigail?"

Abigail cleared her throat. She must be strong, but she was very nervous. It could backfire on her, and the Rabers might evict her from their home, saying that she was lying.

How should she proceed?

"Thank you for seeing me," she stated. "I know you are all busy people. I needed to see you about Christian."

Christian looked at her, his face like thunder. She almost balked, but doggedly continued.

"As you know, Christian and I have known each other a long time," she said. "Since school. I have always liked him as a friend, but lately, Christian has been wanting to court me."

Mr Raber smiled. "Nothing wrong with that."

"No," Abigail continued. "There isn't. But I have told Christian many times that I am not interested in him that way, and he continues to pester me. He doesn't listen to my wishes."

Mrs Raber looked at Christian, anxiously. "Is this true, Christian? Have you been pestering Abigail, when she has clearly said no?"

"She wants to go out with me," Christian blurted. "I know she does! She just needs persuading. Isn't that so, Daed? You always told me that women often don't know their own minds, and need a firm hand."

Mr Raber frowned. "That is not what I meant, Christian. Yes, sometimes a girl takes a bit of wooing. But if a young woman has clearly said no to you, repeatedly, then you must do the honourable thing and accept her decision."

"But...but..." Christian shook his head, colouring. "I know that she loves me, deep down!"

Abigail looked at him, coldly. "That is wrong, Christian," she said. "I don't love you, and never will. I have no desire to hurt you, but you must accept what I say. I don't want to court you. I like you just as a friend." That was a little white lie. She didn't like Christian, at all. But she didn't want to completely destroy his confidence in himself.

"Abigail, your wishes will be respected," said Mr Raber, glaring at his son. "I will make sure of it. Christian will not bother you anymore."

"Thank you," breathed Abigail. She turned to Christian.

"I wish you well, Christian," she said. "I hope that you find the woman that you will marry, one who loves you. But she is not me. I hope we can still be friends. Will you shake my hand?"

She offered her hand across the table to him. He looked at it as if he might refuse, then he grudgingly shook it. Mrs Raber looked relieved.

"I must go," said Abigail, rising. "Thank you all so much for letting me speak, and taking me seriously. It means the world to me."

"God speed, Abigail," Mrs Raber replied. Mr Raber smiled at her.

It was over. Christian would not bother her, again. She knew the Rabers, and that they demanded complete obedience. Christian would not dare to defy them, now that they knew. She would have preferred that he realised by himself, but that might never happen.

She had to protect her life. He had already interfered in her budding relationship with Nicholas. She didn't want him to interfere for a minute longer.

*****

Abigail was feeding the hens when a shadow fell across her.

Fear gripped her. Oh, no. It wasn't Christian back – was it?

She looked around. Then gasped. It wasn't Christian who stood there, but another tall man.

It was Nicholas!

She stood up, slowly. She couldn't quite believe that he was here.

He smiled at her, a bit tentatively. "Abigail," he said. "Your mother said that you would be here."

"Here I am," she replied, then could have kicked herself. Couldn't she think of anything better to say?

"Do you want to go inside?" He asked. "I need to talk to you."

She nodded, leading the way out of the hen house.

They sat at the kitchen table, staring awkwardly at each other.

"I thought..."

"I'm sorry..."

They laughed, as they realised they had both spoken at the same time.

"You go," said Nicholas, looking at her as if he had never seen her before in his life. It made her glow.

"I thought that you didn't want to see me again," Abigail said, biting her lip.

"I thought the same," Nicholas replied. "When you didn't answer my letter."

"What letter?" Abigail frowned. "I never received a letter from you. I wrote *you* a letter, which you never replied to!"

Nicholas shook his head, frowning. "I don't understand. I never received a letter from you. But I did send one."

Abigail stared at him, perplexed. Then understanding started to dawn on her face.

"It must have been Christian," she said. "I didn't realise he was going to that level. He must have been monitoring our mail box. Mamm leaves letters we want to send in there for Daed to collect and send when he gets to town."

"Christian?" Nicholas frowned. "That man who has been pestering you?" He paled, and stood up. "This is going too far. I will go around to his house, this minute!"

"Nicholas, sit down," Abigail said. "It's alright. I have spoken to his parents. He won't be bothering me anymore."

"Are you sure?" Nicholas sat down, slowly. "Because if he ever tries again, he will have me to answer to!" Abigail could see a vein throbbing in his temple. He was angry.

"So you care about me?" She looked at him, shyly.

"I do," he replied. "So much so, Abigail, that I travelled here today to speak to you, even though I thought you didn't answer my letter." He paused, looking like he didn't know what to say further.

"I care for you, too, Nicholas," she said, shyly. "Can we begin again? Like before Christian started interfering in our lives. He told me you had a fiancée, back home."

"He what?" Nicholas looked gobsmacked. "That is an outright lie! I would never have asked you out on a date if I had a fiancée. You didn't believe it, did you?"

"I tried not to," Abigail answered. "But when you didn't reply to my letter, I thought the worst. It was Christian, all along."

"We can begin again," Nicholas said, looking at her earnestly. "If you are willing?" He reached for her hand, across the table. "And God willing, of course."

"Nothing would please me more," Abigail replied. She took his hand. Happiness swelled up within her.

Christian was out of their lives. Nicholas cared for her.

The time for joy was upon them.

THE END

AMISH LOVE'S FORGIVENESS

MONICA MANN

December

The service had been lovely as always but Hannah had been unable to concentrate, her mind bustling with dozens of thoughts. As she followed her fiancé's family from the home of one of the member and into the back area of their farm, she wrung her hands nervously.

"Hannah, are you unwell?" She jumped at the sound of Isaac's voice near her ear.

"Not at all! On the contrary, in fact," she replied, peering at him, confusion coloring her face. "What would make you ask such a thing?"

"You seemed not to be paying any attention whatsoever during the sermon. I believe the Bishop scowled at you at one moment." Shocked, Hannah paused in mid step to stare at her husband-to-be, abruptly holding up the line trekking through the field.

"You must be joking!" she cried and then saw the twinkle in Isaac's gentle hazel eyes.

"Perhaps I am but you must admit that your mind has been elsewhere today. What are you thinking about? I noticed the faraway look in your eye from my side of the room!" Hannah laughed and continued toward the barn where the Fisher family had arranged for lunch following their Sunday worship. The winter had been unseasonably warm and Hannah felt somewhat overdressed in her wool cloak. She wished for snow. It did not feel festive without snowflakes gracing the air.

"Well? What is it that plagues your thoughts? Are you reconsidering our marriage?" Again, Isaac's warm eyes lit up with laughter and Hannah grinned broadly at his jesting.

"Certainly not! I am simply concerned about Christmas," Hannah replied, her thoughts beginning to race once more. It was Isaac's turn to show confusion.

"What of Christmas? It is the loveliest time of year. Surely you can't be glum!"

"Not in the least," Hannah replied as they made their way into the spacious structure to join the rest of the congregation. "I am simply worried I have not prepared properly. I have made presents of all of the children and for my parents but I feel as though I have forgotten someone. Which brings me to the Christmas cards. I am always concerned that I have left out a family. Can you imagine how much embarrassment that would bring to us should I omit a single family? What's more is I set up the nativity scene in the front of our home and I cannot find one wise man and two angels. Now I suspect that Rachel has been playing with them but I have yet to find them and she denies knowing their whereabouts. I must have father whittle some for me or else it will be a disaster!"

Suddenly Hannah felt as though a huge weight had been lifted off her shoulders with the confession. Isaac burst into laughter.

"Oh, Hannah! The things which make you fret do amuse me endlessly. It is Christmastime, *liebchen*. It is not a time of worry and fret. That is for the English. We are only to give thanks and spend time with those dearest to us."

"I know, Isaac, but I cannot help wanting Christmas to be perfect! It is my favorite time of the year. And look! This year we haven't even any snow! It hardly seems proper to even set up a tree without the candlelight twinkling off the snow." Hannah pouted but immediately smiled as the truth of his words struck her. Of course he was right; this was not a time of stress. Their way was that of peace and order, not to be overshadowed by the trivialities which the outside word concerned themselves. It was what made the Amish community so special; the ability to block out the unnecessary and focus on the beauty of the basics in life. Hannah could not be happier. She and Isaac had become betrothed in February and their impending marriage was announced to the community in October as per tradition. They had plans to wed the following winter as per tradition and she could not have hoped for a better mate. Despite their engagement, Isaac continued to act as though they were newly enamored with one another, bequeathing her with beautiful flowers and penning poetry for her, words which made her warm to her soul. She was excited to begin her life with him. It seemed that the wedding was millennia away, not merely a year.

"Ah, Hannah, you may worry but your Christmas spirit is infectious," Bishop Philips told her, overhearing the last of their conversation. Blushing scarlet, Hannah turned to acknowledge him, bowing her head.

"Your sermon was well received today, Bishop," Hannah told him, trying to recover from her embarrassment. "It is a rare treat to hear you speak lately. I'm afraid we miss hearing your voice in service. I am pleasantly surprised you have joined us today."

"Unfortunately, I have had business in other districts as of late but I am happy to be back at home. I haven't had the opportunity to congratulate on your betrothal. Isaac, you have done well for yourself. The Yoder family is well respected in our district. Perhaps you will bless them with a son." The Bishop smiled at the couple.

"Not that the Yoder women are any less hard working than any of the men in our community. How is your family? I do not see your father here today," the Bishop continued, looking about, a sudden cloud covering his brown eyes. Hannah and Isaac followed his gaze. Hannah's mother, Ruth stood speaking with several other women while her sisters, Rachel and Miriam ran through the barn, playing a game of tag with some of the other children. As the three continued to look about, Hannah felt a stab of panic in her stomach. It was unheard of for her father, Mark to be absent from church services. She had spent the previous week in Isaac's district at a family member's home. Hannah had been slowly learning the workings of his father's farm at the insistence of Mark who thought it best she understood the complexities of her husband's land as much as possible. As Hannah's cousins resided in close proximity to Isaac's farm, the transition had been seamless and it allowed for their sweet courtship to continue uninterrupted. This also meant, however, that Hannah was not as informed as to the comings and goings of her own family. Brow furrowed, Hannah excused herself and hurried over to her mother, despite Isaac's reactionary hand on her arm to stop her.

"*Mamm*, where is *Daed*?" she whispered in her mother's ear urgently without preamble. Ruth gave Hannah a reproving look and politely exited the conversation in which she was involved.

"Mind your manners, Hannah!" Ruth Yoder chided her daughter.

"I'm sorry Mammi, I am just worried about him. It is unlike him to miss service. I can't recall one instance prior to this one in fact!" Hannah insisted. Seeing her oldest daughter's distress, Ruth's face softened.

"Your father was away at market in Pittsburgh over the weekend. He was expecting to be back last night but the weather turned so he must have been detained. He will likely be home when we return." Hannah exhaled with relief and returned to her fiancé and the Bishop where she reiterated what she had been told. A bell rang to indicate that the meal was about to be served and they all sat at the long tables set up in the middle of building. Yet as they bowed their heads and grace was said, once again, Hannah felt herself distracted by unstoppable thoughts. This time, however, they were not of snowfalls and wise men. Suddenly she her mind was focussed completely on the whereabouts of her father.

"I don't mind, Hannah but I cannot help but feel you are overreacting somewhat," Isaac informed her as they pulled their carriage toward the Yoder farm.

"He is my father. I must know that he is well, Isaac," Hannah replied.

"*Liebchen*, he has been going to market since well before you were born. I am sure he is well. You will see." Isaac smiled boyishly at her and encouraged the horses onward. Hannah felt an uncharacteristic smidgen of annoyance at his placation. She gave him a sidelong look but said nothing. She hoped he was right but some inherent sense told her something was amiss. Inclement weather or not, Mark Yoder would have been at worship. His devotion to God was his priority, probably above his own health and safety. Hannah knew her father. He would have risked riding in a blizzard to honor his commitment to the community. Her mother had arrived back from the Miller farm with Rachel and Miriam and the pale afternoon light was already becoming dark, forsaking dusk altogether.

"I do not see his wagon," Hannah mumbled as they pulled to a stop. Alarm growing in her chest, Hannah recognized the Bishop's carriage which was parked behind the modest house. Hannah did not wait for Isaac to escort her from her seat and instead was running up the front steps to toward the door. As she flew inside the house, she stopped in her tracks. Her mother was on her knees, surrounded by Rachel and Miriam, a look of shock upon their faces. Tears had slipped from their cheeks to the wood floor. Bishop Phillips stood, solemn faced at the base of the stairs, his hat in his hands, his lips pursed into a fine line. They did not need to speak. Hannah already knew.

January

"Hannah, Isaac came calling again," Miriam told her, pushing open the door to the bedroom where her sister sat brushing her long hair, placing it into sections for braiding. Hannah did not respond. Instead she continued to count the strokes, slowly, meticulously smoothing down the strands.

"Hannah? Hannah!" Miriam strode into the room and snatched the utensil from her sister's grip. The older girl looked up in surprise and instinctively grabbed it back.

"What is it?" she demanded, rising to her feet menacingly.

"Isaac was here," Miriam said again. "He would like you to contact him when you are well."

"I am well, thank you. I am simply busy. With *Daed* in the hospital, fighting for his life, someone needs to help *Mamm* run the farm,

Miriam. I cannot up and run off to help him when Isaac has able bodied brothers there. What does he want from me?" Her words were like a torrent of venom and twelve-year-old Miriam stepped back, shocked at her tone.

"I believe that he wants to know if you're well, Hannah. I don't think he wants you to help him on the farm," she offered, timidly, tears filling her eyes. Hannah was immediately contrite but her anger would not lessen.

"Thank you, Miriam. I will be in contact with Isaac shortly." Her sister immediately retreated from the bedroom, closing the door in her wake but Hannah heard her sister's stifled sob before she retreated down the stairs. Hannah knew that her tone had been unreasonably harsh but she could not seem to alleviate the insurmountable rage which had filled her since the horrendous accident her father had endured a mere month before. The driver who had injured Mark so severely on that lone road heading home from the city had yet to be caught and Hannah knew she would not rest until the person had been apprehended and brought to justice. Christmas had come and gone in an unmemorable blur, still filled with family and friends but in a much more somber tone than the joy of the season typically brought. The family had left the candles lit in the windows well after other members of the community had extinguished theirs, a constant flame for others to keep Mark in their prayers. Hannah remembered thinking that the nativity scene was ruined and she had reprimanded Rachel harshly for playing with the wooden characters, reducing the child to a blubbering mess. Much more than that, Hannah could not recall about holiday. There had been an exchange of gifts but Mark's had lay unopened at the hearth and Hannah did not have any recollection of what she had received. Hannah's mother had continued her duty, tending to the farm and caring for the children and Hannah had stepped in to assist as opposed to joining Isaac. At first, Isaac had attempted to stay nearby, offering his unselfish aide to the Yoder family but eventually

Hannah's increasingly sullen behavior had driven him home to his family's land. Still, he had frequently visited his beloved to see how she was faring. More often than not, Hannah made herself unavailable for reasons no one could comprehend. While she never admitted it to anyone, she blamed Isaac also for her father's fate. *If only he had been more vigilante, heeded my words more carefully when I suggested that something was amiss with father,* she told herself time and again. It did not matter that Mark Yoder had been hit on the Saturday night, well before Hannah had any inkling that there was trouble. In Hannah's grief she was beyond reason and all she had remaining was her intense anger. It was irrelevant whom was the recipient of her rage. It needed to be released and Hannah ensured that it was so. Mark's initial prognosis had been grim. The internal damage to his organs was severe and he had several broken bones. He was still on a life support machine in the hospital where he had been taken following being struck. Hannah could not bear to see her strong, vital father in such a condition and had refused to attend his side despite her mother's pleading.

"Hannah, your father needs you there," Ruth had begged her daughter. "Please swallow your repulsion and spend some time at his side. He can hear your prayers."

"He can hear my prayers from here, Mamm. It makes not difference if I am here or there. I cannot bear to see him in such a state with wires poking out of him. Hospitals are filled with harsh lights and harsher people," Hannah countered. "I will not be any good to him there. He knows I am with him in spirit."

Any amount of argument had been futile and eventually Ruth gave up, attending the county hospital with only her two youngest.

"God will not allow him to be taken from us," Ruth assured Hannah one night, attempting to connect with her distraught oldest child.

"God should not have allowed him to have been struck in the first place!" Hannah had yelled back. "God should have been watching out for him. God should have rendered the driver comatose and on life support!"

There was no point in debating the issue. In her mind, Hannah would not rest until she saw the face of the person responsible for the atrocity writhing in shame, guilt and agony.

<u>February</u>

"Ma'am I understand your anger but there we are doing everything we can."

Hannah's blue eyes flashed but she checked her temper.

"Sir, it has been almost three months and you have absolutely no leads regarding the driver of the vehicle which struck my father. Surely you should be exploring other avenues to catch this animal! Doesn't it concern you that this kind of person is driving on your streets where your children walk?"

"Hannah!" Isaac gently placed his hand on her shoulder as she rose from her chair to confront the police detective at the desk. He turned apologetically to the detective.

"Hannah has been under a lot of stress since the accident," Isaac told the man who nodded understandingly.

"Of course, we fully get that and we sympathize," Detective Adams replied. "I have heard that your father is no longer on life support. We are all very happy to hear that."

Hannah felt her hands clench into fists, her nails digging into her palms.

"Yes, praise the Lord for small favors," she answered shortly, her eyes narrowing, ignoring Isaac's fingers which were now increasing pressure on her shoulder. "However, that does not change anything. Is this why nothing has been done to find the monster responsible? Because he is alive? Next time he may not be so lucky if this person is still on the road!"

"Miss Yoder, I assure you that we are doing everything we can but it is very difficult with the circumstances. There were no witnesses, it was a dark road..."

Hannah threw up her hands. She understood. Mark Yoder was not a priority to these people. He would have to be dead or English for them to care. They were just going to say words until she left them alone. Worried she would not be able to contain a barrage of words threatening to escape her lips, she turned to leave without responding. Hannah heard Isaac apologizing for her rudeness once more but Hannah did not wait for her fiancé. Moments later, he was at her side, breathing heavily from chasing her down the crowded street. Under normal circumstances, Hannah would have been unnerved by the throng of people in her midst. It was not like her to visit town, much preferring the quiet way of her community but it had been months and there had been no advancement regarding the driver who had struck her father. Against her mother's pleas, Hannah had taken it upon herself to meet with the detective face-to-face.

"Please, Hannah, Bishop Phillips has been in constant contact with the police. You must not go and bother them."

"If not me, then who?" Hannah had demanded.

"Go see your father! He needs you!" Ruth implored. But the words had fallen upon deaf ears and Ruth had summoned Isaac to accompany her now wayward daughter into town. Isaac had appeared as Hannah was setting off.

"Hannah! That was rude!" He breathed, struggling to keep up with her brisk stride.

"Well perhaps that's what they need, rudeness. Niceties don't seem to be getting us anywhere."

"Hannah, I'm sure they are doing everything they can – "

"It is not enough!" Hannah snapped. Isaac stopped walking, taken aback by her tone. Hannah had never had occasion to speak to him in such a manner. He watched after the woman he was destined to marry and he wondered what had happened to the gentle, even tempered girl he had courted. He understood she was frazzled, not acting rationally but deep down, he hoped that girl was not lost forever.

<u>March</u>

"Hannah, you have not been at worship in several weeks."

The statement was blunt but not filled with accusation. Bishop Phillips simply stared at her, his brown eyes wise with understanding. She shrugged nonchalantly and did not turn from the hens from which she was collecting eggs.

"God knows where I am," she responded flippantly. Bishop Phillips drew closer to her inside the coop, ignoring the squawking of the animals in his midst.

"It is not simply of God knowing where to find you," he told her, gently. "Worship is a place of community, a place where others can shoulder your burden while asking for the Lord's help."

Hannah reeled around to glare at him.

"What does the community know of shouldering my burden?" she asked. "Can they find the animal who ran down my father like a rabid dog in the street? Have they made him pay penance for the harm he has caused my family?"

A warm, fatherly hand reached her shoulder and the Bishop smiled weakly.

"Perhaps not, child, but your suffering is our suffering also. We grow together and we will support one another. That is what makes us strong. You cannot fight this burden alone."

"I am not alone," Hannah retorted. "I have my family. I have Isaac."

But even as she said the words, Hannah tried to remember the last time she had spent more than a few moments with her betrothed. She could not. She shoved the thought from her mind. It did not matter. The only importance was figuring out who had hurt her father. Isaac would have to understand that her priority was with her father.

<u>April</u>

"Hannah! Hannah!"

Miriam and Rachel's footsteps could be heard reverberating through her bedroom well before the door flew open and the twins appeared. Her heart in her throat, Hannah turned away from the window out of which she had been staring for well over an hour, lost in thought.

"What is it? Is it *Daed*? Is he dead?"

Shocked, the girls recoiled at her words, smiles fading from their lips.

"No!" Rachel cried. "Of course not! Why would you say such a thing?"

In truth, Hannah had been waiting for news of the like and had been since the day he had been hospitalized. Her heart began to slow and she forced herself to smile at her sisters.

"I'm sorry. What is it?"

"He's awake! *Daed* is awake!"

Hannah's slowing pulse picked up speed once more. She flung herself into her siblings' arms and the three rejoiced at the news.

"He is? When did this happen? What did the doctors say?" Hannah whipped the questions at them rapid fire. Ruth appeared in the doorway. Her face was gaunt from exhaustion and emotion.

"He will still need some time to recover in the hospital," Ruth answered. "But his ribs are healing as well as his kidneys." Hannah pulled away from the twins and looked at her mother, her face alight with excitement. *Now we will catch you! Daed will identify the driver and it will all be over!*

"Did he say anything?" she pressed. "Can he identify the driver? Or the vehicle? Does he know who hit him?"

Ruth's sky colored eyes clouded over and she regarded her daughter for a moment.

"Hannah, it is not healthy for you to focus so direly on the driver. God will sort out what to do with him. You must instead think of your father and concentrate on good thoughts." Hannah scowled at her mother.

"I am focussed on *Daed*! That is why I want to find out who did this to him! Why am I met with resistance at every turn? You, Isaac, Bishop Phillips. Am I the only one who cares about seeing justice served?"

Ruth pursed her lips together and did not reply. Hannah continued to stare at her mother.

"Well? What did he say? Did he identify the man or not?" she demanded. Ruth sighed heavily.

"No, Hannah. He cannot speak. He had a stroke."

May

Springtime held the promise of new birth for everyone in the community but Hannah. She found herself tending to chores indoor more and more. Isaac had ceased visiting altogether and Hannah found herself in the police station once a week, hounding Detective Adams mercilessly. Where the women in the community would have typically begun to make suggestions for her wedding, offering assistance and chattering cheerfully of their own nuptials, Hannah found herself almost isolated, something she was quite content in discovering. The feeling of helplessness which had overwhelmed her was becoming a suffocating blanket as more time passed and left her no closer to finding the heathen who had hurt her father. She still had not gone to the hospital to see Mark, despite reports from her family that he was faring quite well. He still had not managed to recoup his motor skills and Hannah did not want the face of a crippled man plaguing her already dark thoughts. She would not rest until someone had paid.

June

"You are attending service."

Her voice was flat and left no room for argument. Hannah opened her mouth to speak but caught the anger in her mother's usually gentle eyes and thought better of voicing her thoughts. Grudgingly, she retreated to her room to ready herself for worship.

The family hosting church services was a neighbor and the Yoder family arrived just as Bishop Phillips rose to speak. He fixated his eyes upon Hannah and began to preach of forgiveness. Hannah closed her ears and averted her eyes. *I will forgive when the driver asks for forgiveness. Not one moment before. And even then, I may not.*

July

He came home on a Tuesday and several members of the community were present to welcome Mark. They brought flowers and honey and bombarded him and the family with well wishes. Isaac and his family had driven in also but Hannah only watched the event from her bedroom window, unable to watch her enfeebled father slowly stumble his way up the steps of the veranda. Her eyes filled with tears but whether they were of guilt or pain, she was not sure. As Mark made his way inside with the help of his wife and two youngest daughters, Isaac lifted his eyes toward Hannah's bedroom window. His own eyes were filled with sadness and Hannah quickly ducked back behind the curtains, not willing to look at him. It had been a long while since they had spent time together and she admitted that she missed his company dearly. She often wondered what he was doing and if he thought of her. The look on his face told Hannah that he did long for her as she did him. Swallowing the urge to run downstairs and beg him for forgiveness, Hannah sat on the edge of the bed. She wondered if anything would ever be the same again.

August

"Hannah! Hannah!"

Rachel almost knocked Hannah over as she barreled into the barn. Hannah looked up at her quickly.

"What is it?"

"*Daed* said his first clear word!" Hannah felt hope swell in her chest.

"What did he say?" she asked, wiping her hands on her apron and following Rachel out of the building, toward the house.

"He said 'Hannah.' He's asking for you!"

September

Progress was swift from that moment onward. Every day, Mark Yoder began to say more. He was required to see a specialist in town to assist him in his walking but Hannah was beginning to see signs of the same, strapping man she had admired her whole life. She found it less painful to be in his presence but she still could not help but feel enraged at his condition. When Hannah did stay at his side, she pressed him for details of the accident. To her relief, he recalled a great deal and Hannah feverishly wrote down the details as Mark remembered, every day adding more to the description. Finally, after three weeks, she had a proper sketch of the vehicle and possibly the driver which she immediately took to the police station. *Now we've got you!* She thought smugly.

October

"Are we still to marry?"

The question startled Hannah as she had not heard Isaac at her back. He had been watching her from the porch as she hummed to herself, picking wildflowers. Oddly, the upcoming wedding had been fresh in her mind for the first time in months. Since delivering the description to the police, Hannah had felt as though they were nearing absolution and a giant weight seemed to have been lifted from her shoulders. She stared in surprise at her fiancé.

"I certainly hope so, Isaac. Are you reconsidering?" She felt faint as she waited for him to answer. Slowly, Isaac made his way down the steps and toward his betrothed.

"I feel as though we have become very distant these past months, Hannah. I wondered if you still wished for us to marry." She met the distance between them and offered him her hands.

"Forgive me, Isaac! I have been consumed with worry for my father. Of course I have never thought for a moment that you and I would not be wed." Isaac eagerly accepted her hands and squeezed them gently, smiling with relief.

"I am glad you have finally decided to forgive and move on," he told her. "I knew the sensible woman I know was in there somewhere."

Hannah beamed back at him.

"It will be very easy to move on once this man is caught! I believe the police will finally catch him now!"

The smile died on Isaac's lips as he stared at Hannah. He realized that she was still consumed with the idea of catching the driver. Wisely, he said nothing but a sense of unease filled his stomach. Would this never end?

<u>November</u>

"You must be very excited with the upcoming wedding, Hannah. It has been quite a year for you and your family. It will be a relief to have cause for celebration over bad times, I would say," Bishop Phillips said after service. Hannah smiled widely and nodded, glancing at Isaac. He smiled meekly.

"Yes, we are looking forward to it. A Christmas wedding may seem a bit ostentatious but it is my favorite time of year and Isaac has been kind enough to indulge my whimsy on this matter," Hannah answered happily.

"Well I think it is a wonderful idea. It will only solidify your union with Christ. I am happy to see your father up and about."

"Yes, he is already back into manning the farm as he was prior to the accident."

"Well that is wonderful news, Hannah. It must certainly alleviate your desire to see the perpetrator arrested. It was not good for you to be so fixated on such negative thoughts for so long," the Bishop told her, turning to nod at other members of the congregation.

"No, Bishop, I can focus on other things now. The police are closing in on the animal now that my father has given them somewhere to look. We will have our justice in due time. I must leave it in their hands now." The Bishop looked at Hannah sharply.

"Your father knows who hit him?"

"He gave a very accurate description of the man, yes," Hannah replied. "But as you say, Bishop, it is in God's hands now. I have decided to focus more on my husband-to-be and deal with the criminal when he is found."

Bishop Phillips nodded, his eyes dark.

"Yes, it is in God's hands," he agreed.

December

The police were standing on her porch and Hannah felt her heart leap into her throat.

"Miss Yoder? Is your father home?" the detective asked her, peering over her shoulder. She nodded eagerly and granted them entry. Mark sat in a rocking chair in the front room. He rose to his feet with an agility he did not possess even two weeks prior.

"Please do come in, officers," he told them, cordially. Awkwardly, the detectives ventured into the humble home and stood in the doorway.

"Have you found the man responsible?" Hannah demanded. "Is that why you're here?"

Mark gave her a reproachful look.

"Hannah, where are your manners? Would you like a beverage?" Both men shook their heads and fidgeted nervously.

"Well?" Hannah demanded when there was silence. "Have you news?"

"Hannah!" Mark chided again but the lead detective held up his hand and nodded.

"Yes, Miss Yoder. We have your man. Someone has turned himself in."

Hannah's face went through a variety of changes; hope, shock and then anger.

"He turned himself in?" she almost yelled. "After one year? What kind of monster lets a family suffer for an entire year before confessing his crime?"

"Hannah..."

"Yes, Miss Yoder but frankly, in these situations, it is extremely difficult to find hit and run drivers. We are very lucky that someone did come forward at all," the policeman interjected. "But I do understand your frustration."

"I doubt it," Hannah mumbled. "Where is he?"

"He is in the county lock up. We would like your father to come with us to see if he can be identified in a line up but he had fully confessed to the accident."

"Who is he? A young, drunk English boy?" Hannah asked contemptuously, already envisioning the short haired punk, smoking a marijuana cigarette. Again, an uncomfortable silence ensued. Hannah stared at the men expectantly.

"Who is he?"

Detective Adams cleared his throat.

"It is someone you know," he said evasively. Hannah exchanged concerned looks with her father.

"Who?" she pressed.

"He is your Bishop. Daniel Phillips."

"Hello Hannah."

Hannah felt her legs turn to jelly as she stared at her much-loved Bishop behind the bars of the county jail.

"It is true," she whispered. "How did this happen?"

"I wish I could explain it to you, child but there is nothing I can say which will take away what you and your family have endured over this year."

"Please tell me what happened," she begged, her eyes filled with tears. The Bishop took a breath and told her the story he had relived in his head over and over since the day it had happened.

He had travelled the road hundreds, if not thousands of times before but Bishop Phillips had not slept more than two hours a night in over three weeks. There had been minor unrest in two of the neighboring districts, some petty squabbling which should have resolved itself but somehow a miniscule issue had become a weeks long debate. He was grateful that he was finally able to return home to his district. The car in which he rode had been a gift from a Bishop in one of the districts who had taken pity upon his constant state of commute. Bishop Phillips had to admit that it was more luxurious than his hard riding horse and cart but he also knew that he should not get too attached.

As the headlights lit the way around the road, his heart leapt into his throat. A doe stood frozen in the road, shocked by the onset. In his exhaustion, it took a few seconds for his reaction time to match up with his vision. He slammed on the brakes and veered to the left of the road, barely grazing the tail of the animal but full on impacting something else; a horse drawn cart. The mare whinnied in pain and shock as the Bishop struggled to steady the still moving vehicle. As all was still, Bishop Phillips opened the door to the car and ran toward the now toppled buggy. Inside lay the still body of Mark Yoder, seemingly lifeless. Bishop Phillips stood stock still, unsure of what to do. I must stay and wait for help, he told himself. Then he remembered the two glasses of wine he had consumed with supper. Slowly, he backed up and slipped back into the car, driving away undetected into the black night.

Tears fell from her lids onto her cheeks as she looked at the broken man before her. She thought of how badly she had wanted him to suffer but all she could think of was how much he had already suffered. He must have wanted to ease her agony a thousand times but had been trapped in his own nightmare.

"I understand that you must loathe me, Hannah. You have every right to feel as such," Bishop Phillips told her, his voice cracking. Gently, Hannah reached between the bars and offered the Bishop her hands. He grabbed them instantly and looked at her pleadingly.

"I forgive you," she said simply.

Christmas

"Oh, Hannah you look beautiful," Ruth told her daughter, embracing her warmly. "I have been looking forward to this for so long!"

Hannah laughed.

"Yes, me too Mammi," she joked and lovingly returned her mother's caress. She looked at herself in the mirror one last time. She vowed to her reflection that with this new start she would forsake all anger and rely on God to give her strength in the worst of times. She knew how fortunate she was that Isaac had been strong enough to stand by her during such a trying time and she would never forget it. She turned and looked at her mother and sisters.

"Are you ready?" Miriam asked, hopping back and forth from one foot to another. Hannah looked around and suddenly her stomach dropped.

"Where is *Daed*?" she asked, feeling a familiar sense of panic seize her. The curtain was quickly drawn and Mark strolled in, his gait strong and perfect.

"I am here, *liebchen*. Do you think I would miss giving away my oldest daughter?" he answered. His voice was slightly slower than it had been but his words were perfectly pronounced. There was no sign of the stroke he had suffered. Hannah exhaled. Everything was right again.

MY AMISH HOME

SARAH HAMPTON

It was cold for a mid-June morning. Anna stood by the county road unaffected by the cool breeze. After all, she was used to the hard winters that Seymour could bring. Despite the sun barely rising, the fields were already chirping and buzzing with life. Life started early in the countryside. Anna fidgeted with her luggage. She was not used to doing nothing during the time of day meant for *work*. However, her cousin picking her up had balked at the idea of doing anything before 8 AM, so here she stood and waited on a Friday morning.

She didn't mind waiting. In fact, she was trying to soak in all facets of her familiar home while she could. It was hard to believe that she would be hundreds of miles away by tonight. *Hundreds of miles.* Whisked away by some sort of electric transportation to a new land. Anna had never ridden in a car before. In her opinion, they made far too little noise and could not be trusted. Still, there had to be a reason for Rumspringa to be a time-honored tradition, right? She had heard of girls who never came back. She didn't understand how anyone could turn on their origins. Her parents had told her they would understand whatever she chose to do, but it seemed clear to Anna that they would prefer she stay. After all, they were getting older. She frequently worried about her father working in the field with his bad back. She had always helped him with his work despite her mother's insistence she learn to do "ladylike" crafts instead. As a kid, she would insist on going to the field with her father and carry his tools around, which did not help whatsoever. When she got older, she proved she could work as long and hard as her brothers. Her mother didn't chide her as often now, but she never gave up offering opportunities. *Wouldn't you like to help me cook for this week's market? I could use some help with this quilt. Oh Anna, don't wipe mud on your dress.* She smiled as she thought of her parents. She would be there for them as soon as she returned. She wouldn't allow herself to be dazzled by city lights and electric buggies.

Speaking of which, her electric buggy was supposed to be here by now.

"Where are you, Brittany?" she mumbled absentmindedly as she tapped her wrist.

There was nothing there, of course. She and her friends had seen English people at the markets angrily tapping their digital watches as they demanded punctuality. This had quickly caught on with the children, and it was now the standard among her friends to sarcastically tap their wrists when informing another person of their lateness. Some Amish did wear purely mechanical watches, but it was fairly rare among their order.

She wouldn't see her friends for quite some time. She sat down on her luggage case as she thought about their gathering last night. She was the only one leaving today. The others were either too young or had already returned from their Rumspringas. So, of course, it was an endless torrent of questions and advice. As the night passed, discussion turned to how things would go for Anna.

"I bet Anna will find some rich prince and he'll whisk her away to his foreign castle," giggled her friend Collette.

"Oh, I would never do that," replied Anna, trying to hide a smile.

Collette followed up, unabashed. "Uh huh. And when you do, do you think he'll let us come visit you?"

"Actually," intoned Catherine, "Anna is far too focused on her studies for that sort of thing. If she doesn't watch out, she'll die an old maid."

Anna laughed, but recognized some truth to the statement. "And is that such a bad thing? It seems like wealthy, foreign princes are often in need of old maids. So, I'll still be in a castle."

Collette pounced on this wording, just like Anna knew she would. "Oh, so you admit you're looking for a prince? My, my. I wonder what Elijah would say to that?"

Elijah Beiler was Anna's neighbor and longtime friend. As children, they had quickly struck up a solid friendship due to their mutual hobbies of playing in mud and climbing trees. He was her partner in crime for every dirty, *boyish* activity her friends didn't want to do. They had remained close as they entered their teens. As one could imagine, this spawned lots of teasing and rumors among Anna's girlfriends, but she never allowed herself to take them seriously. If Elijah had any romantic feelings towards her, wouldn't he have shown them by now? After all, frog catching was hardly the courtship material of fantasy novels.

Anna tried to remain deadpan, but couldn't hide the slightest twinge of annoyance in her voice. "I imagine if he had anything to say about it at all, he would had stayed around longer tonight."

She knew it was unfair to blame him for leaving early. He had to help his father pack for the market tomorrow. Still, the petty side of her felt a little disappointed. It was quite likely this would be the last time they would see each other in a long time. Couldn't he sacrifice a little bit of sleep to stay around longer? Truthfully, her feelings for him had changed over time. As they developed into adults, she had come to view him in a way she didn't think he reciprocated. Her friends never gave up an opportunity to tease her about his boyish good looks, his olive skin, or his muscular, strong body built from working the farm since he could hold a hoe. No one ever believed her, but she didn't really care about that. She liked him because of how close they were. She had shared a lot with him and he always accepted her the way she was. In addition, though Elijah was not a purposefully funny man, he always made her laugh with his deadpan, straightforward statements. Anna had trouble imagining developing the same level of bond with another person, let alone another man. Besides, who else would want a girl who wipes mud on her dresses?

Anna stopped her thoughts there. She was supposed to be annoyed at him. The sun was fully shining now. A few strands of her dark red hair obstructed her view. She blew at them forcefully like they somehow represented Elijah. They fluttered a little bit and fell back. She blew at them again—harder this time.

"You know, if you keep doing that, you'll feel lightheaded."

Anna was never one to scream, but the sudden male voice made her jump. She turned around to see Elijah climbing over the fence on the side of the road toward her. She briefly felt a moment of panic about the thoughts she had been having. She knew she had an occasional habit of thinking out loud. If Elijah had heard anything, it didn't show on his face. He walked up to her, took off his hat, and ran his hand through his dark hair while he eyed her worriedly.

"Are you okay? Your face is a little red. It could be the oxygen deprivation."

Anna quickly composed herself. "Eli. My face is perfectly fine, thank you very much. What are you doing here?"

She looked behind him. There were only cows munching grass in the field. "How did you even get here anyway?"

Elijah blinked. "I walked."

"From the market? That must have been five miles."

"I wanted to see you off."

Anna was pleasantly surprised but didn't let it show. "Why didn't you see me off last night then, like everyone else?" she snapped. "And what about your father's market stall?"

Elijah was unfazed. "It was a slow day and I asked if I could leave early. And, well, you seemed to be enjoying time with your friends last night and we wouldn't have had time to talk."

This was an unexpectedly soft sentiment from Elijah, and Anna couldn't think of a quick response.

"I'm just glad I caught you before you left," he added.

Anna tried to hold on to her annoyance. "Well, you almost didn't. I should be gone by now."

"With Brittany picking you up? You'd be lucky if she's awake by now." He rubbed his right leg distractedly. "Plus, I angered a few cows and had to take an unexpected detour."

At this, Anna had to laugh. She stepped forward to embrace him and they sat and made small talk for a few passing minutes. Something popped into her mind.

"So, what did you want to talk to me about last night?

She could see him visibly tense and his countenance changed. There was a small pause before he answered.

"It's just that you're leaving, and I won't see you for a while…" His speaking patterns were too slow and steady for stuttering, but Anna could sense indecision whirring in his brain.

"Yes. And?"

Elijah continued, "I thought I should tell you…" He paused to think. "That you shouldn't…"

Anna was thoroughly confused. "I shouldn't leave? I shouldn't talk to strangers? I shouldn't learn to dance the can-can?"

Elijah was stone-faced but Anna could sense an inner sigh. Whatever he wanted to say, he wouldn't be saying it today.

"You shouldn't forget to say your morning prayers, that's all." He stood and looked down the road. "It seems as if your cousin does have some work ethic. I believe I hear her car."

With that, he gave a goodbye hug and went on his way. Anna couldn't see a car in the distance, but Elijah always had weirdly good hearing. And she couldn't, for the life of her, think of what he possibly wanted to tell her.

—-

Sure enough, after a short while, Anna could hear the familiar sound of Brittany's red Toyota Camry traveling down the dirt road at breakneck speeds. When it arrived, Anna jumped back and let out an exasperated huff. The window rolled down to reveal her ecstatic cousin, designer sunglasses placed on her perfectly styled brunette hair to show her green eyes twinkling with excitement.

"Do all English people drive like that?" cried Anna.

Brittany laughed, "I'm the best driver in Chicago! You haven't seen the half of it."

Anna sighed. "At this rate, I fear I won't even make it to the city."

Brittany winked and got out to help Anna with her luggage. "Don't be such a worrywart! Trust me. You are in great hands."

She stopped to wave at Anna's family approaching behind her. They had heard the car too and were coming to say goodbye. "Now, hurry up and get in! We have a schedule to keep, you know."

Anna's littlest brother Jakob, with the energy only bestowed upon the quite young, was the first to arrive. He came to a sudden stop upon closer look at the strange large machine of transportation. The look of awe on her brother's face made Anna giggle. She remembered the first time she had seen an "electric buggy".

"Jakob! Don't even think about climbing on that car!" shouted Anna's mother, Abigail.

"But, how else am I going to ride it?" asked the confused 6-year old.

"I'll explain it to you later, son. Get back now. It's time for Anna to go."

The young boy frowned, stepped back, and asked with sadness, "You'll come back soon, right Anna?"

Anna picked him up and held him tightly. "Of course I will. I'll have presents for you too!"

At the talk of presents, Jakob immediately perked up and was back to his cheerful self again. Abigail smiled as each of Anna's siblings said their goodbyes. Her father approached and handed her a small parcel. She looked inside. It was a blue and white quilt she had made when she was 11 years old.

"It might get chilly in Chicago. You wouldn't want to catch a cold." Her father said gently.

Anna smiled gratefully and touched her father's hand. "I'll bring it back with me soon."

—-

The drive to Chicago seemed to go by quickly as she and Brittany caught each other up on their lives. They made several stops along the way, as Brittany saw things that caught her fancy. Soon after they arrived in the city, discussion came to Anna's new job.

"So, basically you'll just assist with office work. You'll organize files, help with scheduling, and basically anything else Dr. Jamison wants." Brittany explained in her trademark fast pace, no wear in her voice even after hours of nonstop talking.

Anna nodded, "Is that what you do?"

Brittany laughed. "No. I don't even technically work there. My firm handles their marketing campaigns. You'll love your coworkers though. They're good friends of mine. You'll like Dr. Jamison too, and maybe his son."

Anna nodded again, mesmerized by the electric glow of the world passing by outside. The sun was beginning to set and the city's neon lights grew brighter in comparison. By the time they arrived at Brittany's condo, the night had completely settled. Anna was feeling exhausted from the ride, but Brittany didn't show any signs of stopping as she unlocked and opened the door.

"Ta da! I didn't have a chance to get a key copied for you, so we'll have to do that tomorrow. Oh, there's the cutest coffeeshop down the street from the locksmith. I've been meaning to try it. We can go there together! Of course, first we'll have to get you some new clothes at the shopping mall."

Anna yawned and sat down. "The shopping mall?"

Brittany gave Anna a bemused look. She knew the Amish knew more about outside life than most people thought. She was always careful not to be condescending. "It's like... A big farmer's market." Brittany said slowly.

Anna laughed, "I know what a shopping mall is. I already have clothes though."

This remark got an alarmed look from Brittany. "Oh, but you don't plan on wearing those out here do you?"

"Well, yes I did."

Brittany spirits looked visibly doused. "Well, okay. I'm sure the clinic has a dress code, though, so we should still get you some office clothing..."

Anna relented a bit. "Oh yes. But afterwards, perhaps we could go shopping for some fun modern styles? You know how clueless I am towards fashion."

Brittany's face lit up instantly, "That would be great! It'll be so much fun. In fact, I may know a mall that's still open now..." She said, already checking her smartphone for opening hours.

"Actually," Anna said quickly, giving a more exaggerated yawn this time, "I'm feeling pretty tired. Do you mind if we just stay here tonight?"

And so they did. Brittany made a pasta dinner for the two of them using packaged foods Anna had never seen. They spent the rest of the night watching old movies. Anna concluded her first night in the city falling asleep on the couch, not as enthused by the technological marvel of television as Brittany had hoped.

—-

The rest of the weekend passed in what seemed like a whirlwind to Anna. There seemed to be no end to the amount of things Brittany wanted to show Anna. They had been friends since they were very young, and got along effortlessly. The city girl took Anna shopping for clothes first, of course. After hours of trying on dresses, tops, bottoms, accessories, and what seemed like every shoe in the store, they finally found a wardrobe that was chic enough for Brittany and sensible enough for Anna.

Anna found that her cousin's energetic nature was infectious, and soon was genuinely excited to do the many things suggested to her. Naturally, this delighted Brittany. More hours were spent meeting her friends and Anna's new coworkers. They seemed to truly be interested in Anna's stories of her Amish life and her observations of the city. During mealtimes, Brittany seemed to insist Anna try a new style of food every time. Anna preferred her mother's cooking, but still marveled at the variety available.

Sunday night, Brittany handed Anna a brand-new smartphone and explained how to use it. She had already added the number for her phone, emergency services, and local restaurants to the contacts. She had also created a Facebook account for Anna. The account had 7 "friends," which Anna imagined to be a lot. Brittany then gave Anna her credit card with Anna's name on it.

When Anna protested, Brittany waved it off and said "I don't have any siblings and I don't plan to have children any time soon. I make more money than I need. I don't have anyone else to care for, and you're like a little sister to me. I leave town pretty frequently, so I want you to be covered. Just in case."

Anna kept the card in her new wallet but told herself she would only use it in emergencies.

—-

Compared to the pace of the weekend, her office job seemed to be in slow-motion. She had carried a few boxes and retrieved a few files, but a large part of her time was spent sitting in a comfortable leather chair. Accustomed to the hard labor of working her family's farm, Anna kept asking if there was more work to be done.

Her coworkers found this funny. "You are working. You're sitting there, smiling at patients who come in, and telling them where to sit. This business would fall apart without you. You are the backbone of this operation, not Dr. Jamison," they said. Overhearing this comment, Dr. Jamison laughed and assured Anna she was doing perfectly fine.

The bell dinged and a tall, well-dressed young man with neatly groomed blond hair entered.

"Hello!" enthused Anna. "Please have a seat. Do you have an appointment with Dr. Jamison?"

The young man gave Anna a smile. "I am Dr. Jamison."

"Not yet you're not," her boss's voice interjected before Anna could react. "Your board results haven't come in yet."

The young man approached Anna's desk so he could more clearly see Dr. Jamison behind her. "Yes, father. I'm aware of that. I'm sure I know what the results are, though. Are you thinking I could have failed?" Now that he was closer, Anna could detect a hint of cologne. The subtly pleasant scent contrasted with the edge in his words.

Dr. Jamison, who had been very open and friendly to Anna, didn't even look up from his paperwork and spoke with an admonishing tone which she sensed was very familiar to this young man. "Yes, Christopher. There is always a chance. One day you'll see beyond your ego and realize that."

The young man took a step back and gave a light shrug at Anna. "Very well. Not Dr. Jamison, then. Just Chris, for the moment. I came to drop off a few documents for the *doctor*. I need to speak with him about them."

"Not now, Christopher. I have to prepare these files and then I have patients. Come back at 4:30," came the reply.

To this, the young man gave a thin smile and left without another word, leaving Dr. Jamison shaking his head. Anna offered no comment, but was surprised at how tense English families could be.

—-

At 5 PM came closing time. Again, it surprised Anna to end the workday so long before sun down. Her new coworkers said their goodbyes, already treating her like they were the oldest of friends. Anna sat and waited on the outside deck for Brittany's car. She was a bit late, but that was not uncommon. A true sign of a newcomer to the city, Anna spent the time looking at the cityscape and passing cars instead of playing on her phone.

About fifteen minutes later, Chris showed up looking for his father. Approaching the building, he could see the lights in the office were already dark and sighed. He walked up to the door, not seeming to notice Anna.

She spoke up. "Oh, I think he's already gone. I'm sorry."

She almost instantly regretted saying anything. Based on her previous interaction with this young man, she expected him to offer a snide comment or disparaging look. However, he just sighed again and sat down in a chair across from her.

"I figured he would be. He knows I have lessons until 5. Lunchtime is the only time we were both supposed to be free." He ran his thin fingers through his hair, partially ruining the perfect streaks.

"Why did he tell you to come back at 4:30 then, if he knows you can't make it?"

Chris massaged his temples. "It's his way of saying he's too busy for me."

Anna was surprised to see a vulnerable side to what she had originally perceived as a highly-strung, egotistical man. Having nothing else to do, she decided to probe further.

"Isn't he proud of you, though? You're going to be a doctor." She hesitated before adding the next part but went ahead. "You don't even look old enough to be one."

The young man looked up at Anna. For a moment, she feared she had angered him but he simply laughed and said "I'm sorry, what is your name again? I suppose I've already offered you mine."

Anna offered out her hand, "I'm Anna. I'm new here."

Chris shook her hand. "Chris Jamison. I can tell you're new." His hands were pale but surprisingly warm.

Anna giggled and he continued, "To answer your question, I graduated from university early and went to medical school afterwards. The medical board also thought I was too young, but agreed to allow me to take the examinations, provided I don't practice until next year."

"Next year?"

"When I turn eighteen."

This confused Anna. "So that means you're only…"

"Seventeen, yes. I get these questions a lot."

Chris was only one year older that she was. She took in his facial structure again. He was older than he looked, then. She probed further. "So you're pretty smart, huh?"

This prompted a laugh. "Some might say so. Others, not so much. In truth, I've just always been a very curious person. I read a lot of books as a child."

This seemed unexpectedly modest to Anna from a man characterized as egotistical by his own father. She felt some admiration for what he had achieved at such a young age. "Wow," she mumbled, thinking about her own life.

He leaned back in his chair, his previous melancholy mood forgotten. "So did my father hire you to guard his door? You look a bit too nice for that."

Anna checked the time on her new phone. "Well, I'm waiting for my cousin to come pick me up, but she's late and she hasn't called."

Chris leaned over a little to look at her phone. "Has she texted? You have an unread message."

"Has she what? Oh!" Anna had forgotten about this feature on her phone. She pulled up her messages, and sure enough, she saw one from Brittany.

Hi Anna!!! How was your first day at work? I can't wait to hear about it. My meeting got delayed and I won't be able to get free for several hours! Sorry. Go out with Mike and Kelly. I'll call you when I'm done! XOXOXO"

This message was interspersed with curious yellow cartoon faces, which Anna took to represent exaggerated emotions. Mike and Kelly were her new coworkers. She looked up at their parking spaces. Empty.

Chris took in the look on her face. "It seems that she won't be here for a while."

Anna got up. "Yeah, she's in a meeting. It's okay. I can walk home."

At this, Chris laughed and shook his head.

"What?" said Anna, defensively.

"No offense, but that would be like a puppy walking in the Amazon. You look curious and trusting. That's a dead giveaway you're new to the city. A perfect target for predators."

The last word brought images of bears and wolves to Anna's mind, but then she understood what he meant.

He pressed on, "Plus, I'm willing to bet you're not quite sure how to get home anyway."

That was true. Anna hesitated. "Well..."

Chis stood up and started walking down the front steps. "Come on, I'll drive you."

Anna stood still. "What?"

Christ kept walking. "I'll drive you. You don't want to take a taxi. They charge double rates to people who look like tourists, which you do. My father clearly isn't here, so I have some free time."

Anna followed him a little bit so she could hear what he was saying. She didn't want to be impolite. However, she wasn't sure if she could trust this complicated young man. As Chris opened the driver door to his sleek black Mercedes, he turned to look at her.

"Come on. You can tell your cousin what you're doing. You'll be perfectly safe."

That's right, Anna thought. *Didn't Brittany say she knew Dr. Jamison's son?* She looked up at the sky. It was cloudy, as it often was in

Chicago. She didn't particularly feel like being caught in the rain. She shrugged internally and ran towards Chris's car. *In the spirit of running around, right?*

—-

Not long after they began driving, drops of rain started to appear on the windshield. Anna breathed an internal sigh of relief. Although she didn't think she displayed any outward emotion, Chris seemed to know what she was thinking and gave her a smile.

"Where do you live again?" Chris asked, pulling up the GPS on his dashboard.

I guess it would be silly to hide that now, Anna thought. "In the 600 North Fairbanks Condos. Have you been there?"

"No, but soon I will," he said, typing in the address with soft, precise touches.

Anna watched him. "You know, I wouldn't know personally, but I've heard it's bad to text and drive."

Chris looked and her and shrugged. "You do it, then."

Anna looked over at the glowing screen on his dashboard. After some trouble, she managed to get the device to do what she wanted. She looked over at Chris, quite pleased with herself.

Chris gave a light chuckle but didn't comment. After a short pause, he spoke again. "So how was your first week in English society?"

She was disappointed "I thought I set up the GPS correctly."

"Oh no, you did well. See?" He pointed to the screen where it said her address.

"Then how—" she started.

"Your clothes. It's your first time wearing them. The scent of the clothing shop is still on them. I didn't think you would have chosen that perfume for yourself, it's a bit bold for someone like you. Plus, you've already told me you're from out of town."

He paused to sip water out of a glass bottle before continuing. "It's not just a new outfit for a new job, either. Every time you lean over, you're instinctively rolling up sleeves that aren't there. You're not used to wearing short-sleeve clothing, but your arms are still tan. Very unusual for a city dweller."

Anna felt a little embarrassed, for some reason. "Maybe I'm just from the country," she challenged.

Chris nodded, "Your accent is slightly southern, but you're not used to any sort of machinery. You subconsciously hold your breath when I accelerate quickly. And why would a girl your age move to Chicago to live with her cousin? You're too young for college. I'm guessing you're on your Rumspringa. How is it?"

Anna took this in. "But how did you know it was the first week?"

He laughed. "Because you check your phone very infrequently for a millennial. My father's clinic has had Amish workers before, and that usually changes after the first week."

Anna found his statements to seem somewhat presumptuous, even though they were factual and things she would freely tell people. "It actually hasn't been a week," she huffed.

This tone made Chris glance over at her again. "I'm sorry. That made you uncomfortable, didn't it?" he mused. "Sometimes I get excited and get ahead of myself. Maybe I do need to see past my own ego."

She decided to encourage this softer side of him. "It's okay. It was true."

He responded with a smile and they drove in silence for a while.

A thought occurred to Anna and she spoke up again. "Did you notice anything else?"

This time, he waited before answering. He pointed to a road sign for a bakery. "You're probably hungry," he finally offered.

Anna hadn't eaten since breakfast and she suddenly felt the pangs of hunger. She looked at her new watch. There was plenty of time before Brittany got off work. She agreed to go eat.

"Did you just guess?" she asked.

"Yes," said Chris, pulling into the parking lot. He decided not to tell Anna he had trained himself to guess a person's last meal from the smell of their breath.

—-

Anna thought about Chris and the bakery as she opened the door to Brittany's condo. She had had an unexpectedly good time. The bakery turned out to be owned by Italians. It was undoubtedly Anna's favorite place in the city so far. She expected herself to return soon. She smiled as she remembered the welcoming nature of the middle-aged couple that owned it. They had greeted her and Chris like old friends and seemed genuinely sorry to see them leave. Truthfully, it reminded Anna of how people were in her hometown. Apparently, Chris was a regular customer there.

She had learned a lot about Chris. As they told each other about their lives, they discovered that they shared a surprising amount of interests. They both loved classical art, piano music, and reading. Chris, who had initially come across as cold and standoffish, was an extremely passionate person. As he had said earlier, he was very curious. This applied to virtually everything. He told her about various authors and their differing viewpoints on a broad spectrum of subjects, including astronomy, medicine, philosophy, art, history, theatre, and literature. She didn't understand all of the terminology he used, but as a curious person herself, it was intrinsically interesting. Chris was pleasantly surprised when she brought up her own theories and questions. He was used to people nodding along and feigning interest. Anna appreciated how he answered her questions and explained things simply without seeming condescending.

When she mentioned this, he said "Einstein believed that if a person couldn't explain something simply, then they didn't understand it well enough." This was followed by a quick list of little-known Einstein facts.

They had stayed much later than she had expected, but Brittany had informed her via text that she had stopped to get a few drinks with friends after work anyway. As Anna rested in one of Brittany's brightly-colored lounge chairs, she was surprised to find that the smile on her face was from thoughts of Chris as much as thoughts of the bakery. She thought fondly of his enthusiasm and charm. *Are all men in the city like this?* she wondered.

As she was thinking about taking a shower, Brittany burst into the room. Her cousin changed out of her office clothing in what Anna thought must be record-breaking speed, all the while talking about her day. In less than a minute, Brittany was reclined next to Anna, dressed in evening wear and sipping a glass of Zinfandel.

"Anyway, enough about me. Your first day at work! How was it? I'm sorry I couldn't pick you up. I'm sure you were okay with Mike and Kelly, though. I think they're dating now. But I thought Mike was gay? Maybe he just dresses well. Which one drove you home?"

She paused to take a drink and Anna picked this opportunity to speak before more questions came.

"My first day went really well. And, actually, Chris drove me home." She realized that she had forgotten to tell Brittany with who gave her a ride.

Brittany paused mid-sip. "Chris Jamison?"

"Yes, him."

She looked up at Anna, her eyes bristling with the excitement of possible gossip. "He's cute, isn't he? Tell me everything."

So Anna did, starting from his office visit to the bakery to the ride home. Brittany listened intently, nodding along to every sentence. When Anna finished, her cousin beamed at her.

"Oh, Anna, that's great! I'm so glad my meeting ran late, now! I wonder, would that be divine intervention? I did throw a penny into the fountain at the mall." She scratched her chin.

Anna wrinkled her brow. "What?"

Brittany sat up and looked at Anna. "It sounds like you two hit it off. He clearly likes you."

Anna was still confused. "You mean, romantically?"

"Yes, romantically! He *likes* likes you. He's usually very involved with himself and doesn't talk much to anyone else. You must have caught his eye. I knew buying that blouse was the right decision!" Brittany looked like she was on the verge of squealing.

This seemed doubtful to Anna. "Well, I don't know about that..."

Brittany went into a neutral expression. "Oh, you don't like him?"

Anna hadn't even considered this. She had just met him, after all. *Life moves so fast in the city*, she thought.

"It's not that. I just..." she stopped, not knowing what to say. She had only felt that way about Elijah, before. She thought about the last time she'd seen him. Although it made her stomach clench a bit, she decided to tell Brittany about her feelings for her long-time neighbor and friend. After she was done, she felt as if a weight had been lifted from her chest.

Brittany nodded, taking this in. "I'd wondered if anything was going on between you two."

"Well, there's not. I don't think he feels that way about me and I don't know anything about Chris."

Brittany stood up and stretched, finally seeming to slow down. "Well, go out on a few dates with Chris and see how you like him. You can always stop."

"Go out?"

Brittany turned to look Anna in the eye. "He did ask you out somewhere, right?"

Anna thought about this. "Well, he did mention taking me to the theatre this weekend."

She told Brittany more about it. As she finished, Brittany excitedly spoke. "That's a date!"

"Is it?" Anna said, flabbergasted.

"Yes! We'll have to decide what you wear! Oh, so little time to shop."

As Brittany started talking to herself about outfit possibilities, Anna thought about what she wanted to do. She was unsure about dating anyone, but she found that she was quite excited at the thought of seeing Chris again. *I'll go,* she decided, *and then we'll see what happens.*

———

The week passed uneventfully except for the weather cooling unexpectedly. The condo was well heated, but it made Anna feel a little warmer on the inside when she slept in the quilt her father gave her. Then, the weekend came and Chris took her to the theatre. The production was *Les Miserables*. She had read the book before, but was awestruck to see the plot re-enacted by the characters' singing voices. The main character, Jean Valjean, was played by a handsome man with a passionate voice. When the story ended, Anna was surprised to find a single tear rolling down her left cheek. Chris, not taking his eyes off the stage, offered her a handkerchief.

As they were leaving the theatre, it was chilly and Chris draped his dark blazer over her shoulders. They talked about the play as they walked back to the car and on the drive back. They shared their favorite parts and he told her about the history involved in the plot. He drove her to the front entrance of the condos and exited the car to open the door for her. He held her gently by the shoulders when she stood up.

"So, what did you think?" he asked.

She didn't think he was talking about the play. "I really had a good time," she replied quietly. She meant it, and offered him a warm smile.

He returned it. "Would you like to go out again next weekend?"

She thought about it. Despite what she discussed with Brittany, she wasn't completely comfortable with courting someone she just met. In her home community, courtships were serious business, and people only began them after knowing the person for some time. However, it seemed that the English use dating as a way of getting to know someone. She really hadn't felt uncomfortable tonight at all. In fact, she was surprised at how relaxed Chris made her.

"Yes," she said, smiling wider. The smile hadn't faded by the time she walked into her condo. Brittany was, of course, ecstatic.

—-

As it turned out, she saw him before that weekend. The following Wednesday, he had come in to see his father after work and they went out for coffee afterwards. There was a Starbucks coffeehouse on the street of her workplace, but Chris had turned his nose up at that. He took her to a hole-in-the-wall place with excellent pastries and beautiful latte art. She had always liked dark coffee, but she found that she was becoming attached to the more ornate espresso drinks popular among English girls.

They still went out that weekend. They went out next weekend too. The following month flew by as they saw each other more frequently. She felt as if he was trying to take her to everywhere in the city. They went hiking, boating, and even jet skiing once. He was teaching her how to drive, and she was doing surprisingly well. He tried to sign her up for a gym, but she just couldn't see why people would pay money to lift heavy objects.

She remembered one time in particular. They had planned to go see an outdoor concert in the evening, but a sudden downpour had caused the band to reschedule. He suggested they go to his house and she agreed. She discovered he lived slightly outside of city limits. They were soon pulling into the driveway of an enormous building on top of a hill.

"What part of this is yours?" she asked, craning her head to see how high the manor went.

He laughed. "All of it. Well, my family technically owns it, but I'm the eldest of two heirs."

He explained that his family members were mostly wealthy businessmen in the pharmaceutical industry. Only he and his father were currently doctors. His family has supported him through medical school, but he wanted to eventually break off and make his own living. This was not a popular decision among his family, and led to tension between him and his father.

Chris opened the front door for Anna and she walked in. She took in the beautiful architecture of the convex ceiling. Chris strolled in to the dimly lit area and pointed to a piano at the far end of the living room. It was illuminated by the light of a large window. Anna could see droplets of the rain sticking to the window, casting wide shadows within the building.

"This is where I've been spending a lot of time since I finished school," he said, sitting down in front of it. He gestured to Anna to sit next to him.

The music he played was dark and haunting at first. Each note, already chilling, rang throughout the spacious chamber, adding to the macabre feeling. Anna shivered, even though she was perfectly warm. The melody soon slowed and became melancholy. The tempo seemed to match that of water droplets slowly dripping off a rooftop after a large storm, adding a mere trickle to the flood that came before. The song transformed once more into a brighter emotion. Anna tried to pinpoint what it was. It wasn't quite happiness. She realized it was *hope*. The song was about hope.

When he finished, she spoke first. "It's beautiful. What is it about?

Chris continued to play an improvisational melody. "Addiction. It's an addict's tale. I was first inspired to write it when I studied the effects of drugs on people in school. It made me start my research into curing addictions."

"I thought you were still taking piano lessons?"

"I am. I'll never be too good to learn."

They didn't say much afterwards. He played music late into the night. Anna listened and watched the raindrops on the windows.

—-

Anna woke up bright and early the next day. She was still dazed from last night. She wasn't quite sure where their relationship was going, but she liked him for sure. She thought about his goodnight kiss last night and wondered if it was a dream. She could still feel the tingle of his warm lips on hers. She could still smell his pleasant scent as he leaned in and put his hand on the side of her face. Surely it wasn't a dream. The kiss was gentle and cautious—sweeter than she would have expected from him. She was smiling absentmindedly as she walked into the kitchen.

"I take it you had a nice time with Dr. Jamison?" Brittany inquired slyly.

Anna made a face. "Don't call him that. I always think of Chris's father instead."

Chris's board results had come in. As he suspected, he did not fail. However, he still had to wait a year before beginning an internship. Anna sat down. "I did have a wonderful time, though. I think I am beginning to like Chris," she blushed.

Brittany laughed. "You'd better get ready because Chris called and asked you to breakfast this morning. It seems he likes you too. "

"Oh, he called you?"

"Well, he tried getting a hold of you… but somebody never answers their phone," Brittany said pointedly as she walked out of the kitchen with her morning smoothie.

Anna dashed for her phone. Sure enough, she saw a couple of messages and a missed call from Chris. She smacked her forehead in exasperation. "Why is it so hard for me to remember this walkie talkie telephone?" she mumbled angrily.

Brittany chuckled and called from the living room. "It'll probably take you some time to get used to. Don't worry! Chris understands. He wasn't upset at all. We just made fun of you for about 10 minutes. "

"At least my struggles are entertaining to you two," Anna deadpanned.

"They are! I'll be thinking about them all day at work. I must get going now. You better get ready. He'll be here in 30 minutes." Brittany was quickly out the door and the ding of the elevator could be heard shortly after. Anna decided to wash up and put on her brand-new navy blue dress. She slipped on her sweater and shoes and almost immediately heard a knock at the door. She swung it open, already elated.

"You have good timing! I just put my shoes on and—"

Anna stopped as she stared into familiar brown eyes. *Chris doesn't have brown eyes,* she thought. Instead, a disheveled, exhausted-looking Elijah stood in the doorway.

Before she could react, he spoke. "Anna I need you to come with me." There was urgency in his voice.

"Elijah! What are you doing here? Is something wrong?"

Elijah spoke quickly, which was unusual for him. "Your father has had an accident. He's been admitted into Mercy Hospital St Louis. Your mother is there with him. The others had to stay home. Your mother asked me to come get you. She says she hears your father say your name at night. His spine is injured badly. They will operate on him soon. We have to hurry."

Anna stood there in shock. Elijah tugging on her hand snapped her back to reality. Unable to process everything, she grabbed her bag and followed Elijah outside. There was a taxi waiting for them.

"What happened, Eli?" she asked as they got in.

Elijah explained while the driver pulled onto the highway. "Our barn was damaged in a storm a few days ago. Some raccoons and coyotes have been trying to get in and attack the livestock. When we had to miss the market, your father came by with your brothers to help us with the repairs. I can't tell you what a godsend their help was. Halfway through, it started storming again. Harder this time. Your father was in the beams when the structure began to collapse. We tried to get to him in time, but the structure fell a few seconds later. Levi was crushed in between the beams. We had to get the lift to pull him out. He was still holding up when they drove him to see Dr. Kimberly, but she sent him to Mercy as his condition worsened. I went with your mother there. They figured it would be faster than mail if I went to get you. So, here I am."

Anna took this in quietly. She was known for being calm in emergencies. "Thank you for caring for my mother, Eli. My family needs our support right now. You were right to get me."

The remainder of the drive was silent until they pulled into an airport parking lot.

"We're flying?" Anna turned to Elijah with a start. It was highly uncommon in their order, but it was allowed during emergencies.

Elijah just grabbed Anna's hand. "Just stay near me. I'll keep you safe. I promise."

Anna nodded as a calm washed over her. She hadn't seen him in a while, but Elijah always meant what he said. She had faith that God had sent him to bring her back.

Elijah took care of checking in and was with her through the entire ordeal. His father had flown once before and had taught him the basics, in case he ever needed it. Anna had little time to process the procedure.

Everything was happening so suddenly; it felt like she wasn't part of reality anymore.

They soon boarded the plane and were on their way to St Louis. Elijah was still holding Anna's hand as they flew. She subconsciously rested her head on his shoulder and soon drifted off to sleep, still tired from last night. Despite the urgency of the situation, she felt at peace flying through the clouds with this man that she'd known since childhood.

As Elijah watched her fall asleep on his arm, he couldn't help but feel content. He leaned back and let the satisfaction and happiness wash over him. He hadn't felt this since Anna left. He hadn't mentioned it, but it was actually his idea to get Anna himself. Her mother had been too distraught to think about much. She had no idea how to reach Anna. After he convinced Abigail that he could bring her back, he was on the next flight to Chicago.

He watched her chest rise and fall as she breathed. *I have to tell her, but not yet,* he thought. She was already going through a lot. He didn't want to overwhelm her. He decided to just enjoy the moment. He looked at the woman he had loved for years. He knew he wanted to be with her anywhere she went. Hand in hand. *I love you, Anna.*

—-

Anna sat in the waiting room as the surgeons worked to save her father. He had been unconscious when they arrived, but she held his hand and spoke with him regardless. She was convinced he could hear her, and her thoughts were confirmed by squeezes from his hand. She had held it until the aides came to take him to his operation. She now looked at a text message from Chris on her phone. She had sent him a hurried message about the situation as they boarded the plane. She looked at his brief response.

Okay. I'll be there soon.

Be there soon? she wondered. *He's coming to St. Louis?* Sure enough, he showed up 30 minutes after she did. However, he didn't say much. He asked Anna some specifics about her father's condition. She didn't know, so he donned a lab coat and went to speak with the doctors. She could hear the whispers from the hospital staff. Apparently, he was somewhat famous among the medical community for graduating medical school in his teens. *Why couldn't he tell me more about my father? Why can't any of the doctors do that?* She looked over at Elijah, who was finally asleep after three days awake. *Without him, I wouldn't have known for several days.*

The sound of the operating room exit slamming open jolted him awake. Chris, in surgical attire, walked out with a clipboard in a hurried manner.

"Good news. There was a time when we thought he wasn't going to make it, but he somehow rallied and got through the woods. Your father is going to be okay."

He pulled off his mask. "They wouldn't let me touch him, of course. Not enough experience. After some convincing, they allowed me to observe. I've seen cases like this before. He's lucky to be alive. How much he'll recover remains to be seen."

Anna's eyes were wet with joy. Chris moved to sit next to her, but Elijah suddenly jumped up.

"So that's it? Mr. Miller will definitely be okay?"

"Yes. They're finishing up with him right now, but I wanted to come out and tell you." Chris said slowly, with Elijah already furiously pumping his hand in a firm handshake. He rubbed his thin fingers afterwards, wondering who this man was.

Elijah spoke with gratitude. "Thank you very much, doctor. We are forever in your debt."

"Of course. Who—"

Chris was cut off as Elijah moved in front of Anna. "Anna, now that we know your father will be okay, there's something I have to say.

It might not be the best time, but I can't wait any longer. I should have told you the day you were leaving, but I couldn't. I wanted to tell you on the plane, but you had too much on your mind. But I have to tell you now."

And, so he did. He told her that he had loved her for many years now. He talked about the adventures and laughter they had shared from since they were very little. He described the moment he knew he wanted to spend his life with her. He talked about the many times he almost told her his feelings.

"I wanted to tell you sooner. I should have told you sooner, but I was too worried about losing you. But since you've gone, I've felt this burning fire in my gut because you didn't know. It wasn't until then that I realized I had to tell you, regardless of your response."

Anna stood in shocked silence. She was already very emotional from the news about her father. She wondered what Elijah meant by "too much on her mind," as there was still quite a lot. He was usually a man of few words. She must have had these words in his mind for a long time.

He took her hand in his and held it. "And I mean that. I would never pressure you to do something you don't want. To *feel* a way you don't feel. I just wanted you to know, and tomorrow seemed too far away."

Anna stared at him unblinkingly. She felt paralyzed by the hurricane of emotions whirling through her. She wondered if Elijah knew this. She finally managed the strength to glance over at Chris. His face was unreadable, but he set down his clipboard, threw up his hands, and walked out.

"Elijah, I..." she managed.

He patted her hand. "You don't have to say anything right now. Think about it. Or don't. Don't feel obligated to do anything. No matter what happens, I'll love you. I'll love you as a life partner or as a friend, depending on what you need. Just take your time."

With those words, he let go of her hand, put on his hat, and strolled away as if nothing happened.

—-

The next two months were a complex time for Anna. She and her mother were overjoyed at her father's recovery, but he was still bedridden for the foreseeable future. In addition, the steep hospital bills suddenly left the family in debt with the primary breadwinner unable to work. Anna responded to this by taking on a second job at a nearby diner. Days passed by in a blur, but not the kind that comes with fun times. For Anna, this was the blur of sleep deprivation and exhaustion. After a long day at the Jamison clinic, she threw herself into washing dishes and sweeping floors. She often didn't come home until well after midnight, sometimes catching a worried look from Brittany before collapsing on her bed. After a few short hours of sleep, her day would begin again.

Brittany had insisted upon helping with the family bills. Her initial financial support was how the family avoided bankruptcy. However, much of her assets were tied up in physical investments and stocks, and couldn't be quickly liquified. Still, Anna couldn't thank her enough and promised she would repay her. She had already used her previously untouched credit card to make her way back to Chicago.

Anna knew the grind of hard times and took it in stride, but she worried her body couldn't hold on much longer. Every night, she prayed that she wouldn't become seriously ill. She needed to be healthy to work for her family. However, she could feel herself breaking down. She had already developed a foreboding cough that wouldn't go away.

Of course, there was also what happened in the waiting room. In her rare moments of free time, she worked on a letter she was writing to Elijah. They had a lot to discuss. She had written many versions, but most of them ended up in the trash. She just couldn't find a good way to say what she felt.

She also needed to talk to Chris. He had effectively disappeared. Anna tried to make time to see him, but their schedules never seemed to be compatible. The few times she had seen him were at the office, and he always left in a hurry. Working in what seemed like despair and hopelessness, she really wished he were there to offer reassurance. Brittany had angrily called him a "fair-weather lover."

When Anna suggested he simply didn't have time, Brittany waved it off. "No, Anna. That's the oldest, flimsiest excuse boys will give you. The truth is that they will make time if they want to give you time."

This only served to further depress Anna.

—-

Anna got out of the car and waved goodbye to Kelly, who had dropped her off. Autumn seemed to come early in this city. Although it was still warm during the day, she could already see golden brown leaves skating across the sidewalks as the wind blew them through the city. The cool wind exacerbated her cough, so she walked quickly towards the condominium's front door. She only had an hour to shower and change before her shift at the diner. As she walked through the glass doors into the lobby, she saw a familiar face. Chris stood by the back wall, near the mailboxes.

He took a few steps towards her. "Anna, we need to talk."

"Hm. No. You're probably busy. I wouldn't want to keep you." She turned to walk towards the elevators.

He blocked her path and she tried to go around him. He moved again. This continued for a few moments. "Anna, I'm leaving," he finally said.

She stopped. "What?"

"To Singapore. Next week."

When Anna didn't respond, he continued "I found a clinic there that would let me work before I turn eighteen. They like the research I've done about addiction treatments and want to be a part of it."

"Good for you. Is that all you came here to do? To boast?" She headed towards the elevators again.

"Well, no. I actually came to give you this." She stopped and turned around. He took a thin envelope out of his peacoat and handed it to her.

"What is this?" she asked, as she opened it. It was a check for the remainder of her hospital debt.

"It's from Brittany too," he said hurriedly as she tried to angrily shove it back into his hands.

"What?"

"Well, actually it's from the bank. We had to work together to get a loan. It's in our name, so you can pay her back over time. This way, you don't have to work yourself to death."

Anna looked at him. "Brittany says you're a fair-weather lover."

Chris smiled thinly. "I know. She called to chew me out multiple times. She really cares for you."

Anna took out the check and stared at it. "Why did someone like you need to get a loan anyway?"

He looked away. "Well, the truth is..." He paused to chuckle. "The truth is I'm kind of broke at the moment. My family really didn't approve of my move to Singapore and have threatened to cut me off. They want me here to run their businesses. My father was the only one that supported my decision. It was only because of him and your cousin that we were able to get a loan at all."

Anna felt some pity for him. "That's too bad. I had no idea."

He waved it off. "Don't feel bad. I suspected this would happen and did it anyway. I just came here to drop off the cashier's check with Brittany, but she said I should give it to you personally because I owe you an apology. I really am sorry, Anna. I genuinely have been busy preparing for Singapore, but I should have been there for you."

Anna looked down at her shoes. "I'm sorry you had to hear what Elijah said. He didn't know who you were." She looked up at him and took a breath. "About that..."

He closed the gap between them and grabbed her gently by the shoulders. "You don't have to explain it. A few moments after that Amish boy spontaneously confessed his love to you, I knew how you felt. I've seen how you look at me, and I've seen how you look at him. There's no comparison."

He looked away as he continued. "I will confess that I was a little disappointed at first, but I recognized the passion and fever in his voice as he talked about you. He had hope for a life with you. Everyone needs hope."

Anna didn't say anything, but her smile told Chris everything he needed. He took a step back and returned it. "Of course, I won't forget our time together. I'll always be here if you need a friend. That is, if you want to stay in touch?"

Anna's smile widened. "Yes, I would."

—-

It was surprising to Anna how quickly life could change. With her family's financial troubles temporarily relieved, Anna didn't need to work her second job. This allowed her body to finally get enough rest again, and her cough began to clear. She still worked hard, of course. She created a payment plan for repaying Brittany and followed it. Additionally, she had received news that her father was walking again and was expected to make a full recovery. Anna felt as if the sun had risen in her life after a long, cold night.

She also had time to finalize a letter to Elijah. She sat down and wrote from her heart. After she was done, she read what she had written:

Dearest Elijah,

I was delighted to hear the news about Dad's progress. Please continue to watch over him. I know he'll be itching to get back to work, but he must take it easy.

I am sorry it has taken me so long to write to you. I could blame it on being busy, but truthfully... I guess I just wasn't sure how to say how I felt. I've had that problem with you since we were kids, and I guess you know how I feel. Sometimes we're still looking for the words to say...

Why didn't you tell me sooner, Eli? Of course I feel the same way. I never dared hope that you shared my thoughts. I suppose I feared that if I told you first, that hope might be gone. I know now that hope is never truly gone. It stays with us, and if we dare to embrace it, it shines a light on the path God meant for us to walk.

I must say that we will need to work on your conversational timing, though. What a moment you chose to say those things!

I'll need to stay in the city a while longer to work, but after that I am coming home. I'm coming home, Elijah. I have loved Chicago and I love Brittany, but this experience has only helped me realize where I need to be. I look forward to seeing you again.

Forever yours,

Anna.

She smiled and folded the letter into an envelope. As she walked down to the mailroom, she thought about her mother, father, and siblings. She thought about living a life with Elijah and raising a family of their own. She laughed as she thought about what her friends would say about that. There was no doubt in her mind that was her home. She would be there soon.

AMISH SWEETHEARTS

ERICA FANNING

Isaac Yoder couldn't remember a time in his life when he felt so alive. It wasn't his first Sunday night out with the other Amish teenagers. In fact, he was coming up on his 18th birthday, but this night was different. There was singing and Bible reading, as well as fellowship with the young women to find a potential mate, but this time was different. His best friend since 3rd grade, Miriam Hershberger, was there for the first time. She had just turned 16. He had liked some of the other young women well enough, but when Isaac saw Miriam that night, with the twilight coming in through the church windows and the candlelight dancing off of her loose golden locks that never really stayed in her head covering, he suddenly had different feelings for her. He might have imagined it, but he was sure she had looked his way a few times that night, and it was more than just a friendly look.

His friend Joshua noticed it too. "Look at Miriam over there. She looks beautiful." He had leaned closer so that no one else could overhear. Isaac nodded. "I know how much you like her." Isaac scoffed lightly. Joshua slapped him hard enough on the back to take his breath away. "Go talk to her!"

Joshua Hostetler was Isaac's best guy friend. Isaac, Miriam, and Joshua were nearly inseparable. Even though Miriam was two years younger, she always presented herself as the oldest of the three. Even in schoolwork, Miriam could have been two grades ahead, but her father wouldn't allow it.

Miriam's father, Jacob Hershberger, was absolutely opposed to Isaac courting Miriam. Had Isaac asked yet? No, but the men in the fields talked. Many times Isaac was sure they thought he couldn't hear them, but he heard every word: Jacob desired for his eldest daughter to marry none other than Isaac's friend, Joshua. Her father was insistent that he knew what was best for his daughter. Jacob only allowed Miriam to come to the Sunday singing because she had incessantly begged him to let her be a part of the youth group since her two best friends had both been there for two years. Rumor was that Joshua had already started dating Miriam, but when Isaac asked him about it, he denied it. Tonight was proving that more than any words.

The Amish (who call themselves Plain) have what they call *Rumspringa,* or more literally, "running around." It's a time for youths ages 16-22 to find a suitable spouse. There is a common misconception that it is also a time for Plain youths to experiment with the English (non-Plain) world. Though they have the option to do so, *Rumspringa* is more for finding a spouse than for experimenting with the world. However, Isaac had been entertaining the idea of leaving the Plain community to join the Army. The only people who knew of this were Miriam and Joshua. There was something about being in the Army that really intrigued Isaac. He had seen soldiers come through their community on tourist trips and had asked them what it was like. Many of them had been overseas and seen things Isaac only dreamed of: new worlds, new cultures, and new people. The only thing really keeping Isaac in the comfort of his community was the potential to date and marry Miriam.

"I think I'm going to ask Miriam if I can take her home," he finally said to Joshua.

Joshua chuckled, "If you hadn't said that, I would've done it."

Isaac smiled wryly. Ever since they were young, Isaac and Joshua were always in competition; to many it was even a surprise that they were such good friends. Isaac believed it was because of Miriam they were such good friends. She had broken up more than one fight and was always keeping the peace between the three of them.

"This is one thing I won't let you win."

"What? Why not?" Joshua looked affronted. "We can't even have a little friendly competition for a girl? And especially for a girl we've both liked since we were 8?"

Isaac shook his head. "Nope. I thought we had discussed this. I'm the best option for Miriam."

"Oh really? Well Mr. Hershberger doesn't seem to think so. You and I both know the rumors are for Miriam and me. I'll make a deal with you; if Miriam accepts your offer, then you can have her." Isaac shot him a skeptical look.

"That's really nice of you... but why would she say no?"

"Well, my friend, you may not realize this, but Miriam likes me better." Isaac rolled his eyes.

"Why does the world always revolve around you and your stories of a love triangle?"

Joshua held up his hands. "Hey, it's what sells these days. And I would know, since I work at a bookstore in town. But don't worry, I'll let you try to win her hand. But you and I both know, it's her father's heart you'll really have to win. So good luck." Joshua slapped him on the back again before rising from his seat. "I'm going to ask Rachel Swartz if I can take her home." He winked as he walked away. Isaac watched him leave. Rachel Swartz's father was just like Miriam's: very stubborn and wanting one person only for his daughter. In this case, that person happened to be Isaac Yoder. It occurred to Isaac in that moment that Joshua may have been trying to make him jealous, but you can't make someone jealous that doesn't even have feelings for a certain person.

Isaac sighed as he built up the courage to stand up and walk over to where Miriam was sitting. As he moved toward her, the girls around her steadily grew quieter and began speaking in more hushed tones. "Miriam," he half-squeaked as she turned to look at him. He cleared his throat before finishing his request, "May I take you home tonight?" There was suddenly a flurry of giggles from the group sitting around her.

"I'd love that," she replied sweetly. He offered his hand to help her up and began leading her toward his buggy. He had recently purchased the buggy from Rachel Swartz's father. Although "purchased" would be the wrong word, since Caleb Swartz gave it to Isaac as a sign of good faith that he would "make the right choice" in his future wife.

Isaac pushed all of that out of his mind as he helped his best friend into the carriage. He ran around the other side and got in and off they went toward Miriam's home.

About halfway there, Miriam finally spoke. "You can't take me home."

This caught Isaac off-guard for two reasons: one, she had been completely quiet until that point and it had startled him; and two, it didn't make sense.

"Why not?"

"Because," she barely whispered above the clopping of hooves, "my father will be angry with me if I bring anyone other than Joshua Hostetler home."

Neither of them spoke for a few minutes, but Isaac led the buggy toward their favorite secret spot. This spot was known only by Isaac, Miriam, and Joshua. The three of them had found multiple places to hide away from the adults over the years. This particular place was right on the edge of the community, very close to a busy road, but far enough away that it wasn't so distracting in the quiet moments. This spot was Isaac's favorite hiding spot. It was in that spot that he had tutored Miriam in her arithmetic and helped her learn how to read. It was where they had read countless Nancy Drew books in secret, and also where they would get together to talk about their fears of the future and their hopes for each other. Before life got to be about who to marry and where to work, this was where they felt the most at home. Isaac felt it was the best place to go since it had such a deep meaning for them.

As they approached the spot, he had to get out of the buggy and lead the horse to a tree where he could tie the beast up safely. Isaac picked a tree that was far enough away from the road that passersby wouldn't see the buggy and accidentally think something had happened. They were hidden quite a ways into the wood for that.

Isaac helped Miriam out of the carriage and led her through the wooded area to the clearing. It had been awhile since Isaac had been here—almost a year at least—but everything was just as he remembered it: a small circular clearing, not more than 10 feet around with three small logs around the edges of the clearing and a flat-top rock to make the fourth sitting spot. There was an evergreen tree on the north side of the clearing, and that was where they had hidden many of the "forbidden" Nancy Drew books in wooden boxes Isaac and Joshua had made in their free time at home. The entry point was on the south side, and there was a small piece of cloth with Miriam's initials on it. Isaac was never really sure why she had done that, and she had never explained herself... and that was just another reason why he loved her; she did things without anyone's approval.

The sun was almost completely gone, but the Sunday night gathering would last for some time before anybody's parents would start to get suspicious about where Isaac and Miriam were. "Remember the last time we were here together?" Miriam asked. Isaac smiled, recalling that day as if it had just happened yesterday.

"We all showed up here at the same time. You had had a rough day at school and Joshua and I just needed a break from working. We thought we could get away and just play some cards, but then you showed up." He looked into her eyes. "It was in that moment that I realized I wanted to marry you someday."

Miriam furrowed her brow as she said, "That was the day? I was a mess; I was crying like a baby—"

"No, you were wailing like an old widow." They laughed at the thought. Miriam sat down on a log.

"Yeah I was." She chuckled, but to Isaac it sounded like the birds were waking up in the morning. She began speaking again, but he could only focus on her features. Her beautiful golden hair was now freely flowing, as she had taken her head covering off after declaring that they couldn't go to her house. What she said was only mildly important to how she carried herself and how mesmerizing she was. Her green eyes fit well into her oval-shaped face. Her petite nose reminded Isaac of one of the glass baby dolls that his mother had on display at home. When she smiled, all he saw was perfectly white teeth behind full pink lips.

"Did you ever realize how beautiful you are?" He didn't even stop to think that she might have still been in the middle of a story.

"What?" She seemed a little surprised at the sudden outburst from her friend.

"You're beautiful," he declared.

She looked at him awkwardly then said, "I thought this was the time when we were supposed to talk all night long. We are basically dating, right?"

"We are talking. You're telling me stories, and I'm telling you how beautiful you are."

She scoffed. "The whole situation sounds a little one-sided to me."

Isaac shrugged. "Well, it worked. You're not telling me stories anymore."

Miriam gasped in feigned offense. "Oh, I see how it is. You don't even want to listen to how Mr. Troyer came into the shop and flirted with me? It's really quite entertaining." Isaac laughed with her. This was going to be a great night.

"Go ahead and start your story again. I'll be good and listen this time, I promise."

That night was the springboard for a whole slew of secret adventures together. Isaac and Miriam grew closer together in ways they didn't know was possible. Isaac felt like he was on the highest mountain and nothing could touch him. For the next three weeks, they would meet in their secret spot late in the evenings and talk into the middle of the night.

One night in particular, the conversation led to the future.

"Hey Isaac," Miriam started. "What do you think about the future?" She looked at him. "Do you think we end up together?" He thought long and hard and then chose his words carefully.

"I don't know what the future holds for us," he spoke slowly. "But I do know one thing." Isaac looked deep into her eyes. "I don't want to live my life without you." There was a long moment of silence as they looked into each other's eyes. Finally Miriam broke the silence again.

"Do you want to go into the Army?" Isaac looked away. The answer was, he really wasn't sure. And he told her as much.

"Those Nancy Drew books made me want to explore the world outside, and the soldiers that came through here recently made me just want to travel. So, I'm not sure if I would just travel or join the Army."

"Well," Miriam began. "You know how our Lord feels about war."

"Does He really feel that way though?" He looked up at her again. The moon was very bright that night and it made Miriam look almost angelic. He continued with his thought despite the minor distraction. "There's war and fighting all throughout the Bible. Even Jesus Himself said He came to bring a sword, and to bring families against each other."

"Do you really only want to fight because you think it's OK? Is that how you're justifying all this in your mind? Any time you take a life, that's blood on your hands that you'll have to answer for."

"Yeah, but Miriam, it's not just about the killing. It's about saving the lives of those that can't fight for themselves. Aren't you always going on about how you want to do what's right and bring justice to people's situations?"

Miriam was incredulous at this point. "Of course, but not by getting myself involved in some war and killing people. I want to help people *here,* in my community. I want to tutor young children... like you and Joshua helped tutor me." Her face softened as she leaned toward him, her voice almost a whisper. "Isn't that enough?"

Miriam was so close, Isaac would've agreed with anything she said at that point. He could feel her breath on his face, smell her sweet, natural scent. "Yeah," he breathed out, before leaning in to close the distance between his lips and hers. As soon as their lips touched, something like a fire shot through Isaac's body and he instantly wanted more. Every nerve in his system and every hair on his body seemed to be standing at attention, but in the next second, he was left breathless and confused. Miriam had pulled away.

"No," she stated firmly. "I can't." She stood to leave.

"Wait, Miriam." Isaac stood to follow her. "Don't leave. I'm sorry." He wasn't sure why he was apologizing, since he didn't really start the whole ordeal.

Miriam kept walking toward Isaac's waiting horse and buggy. "I need to leave. Please take me home."

"Wait, Miriam," he said again, more firmly this time as he reached out to grab her. She spun around, and what Isaac saw stopped him. She was crying.

"Please just take me home. I can't be with you. I can't keep playing this game of pretending to be into someone but really loving someone else."

Isaac released her arm. "Who else are you interested in?"

"It's not who I'm interested in, it's who my father *wants* me to be interested in. I can't keep pretending anymore." She looked into his eyes, and he had this sinking feeling that this might possibly be the last time he would get to talk to her for a long time. "Isaac, I love you, but if you want to date me, you *have* to get permission from my father." She turned around to continue walking toward the buggy.

"OK," he said finally. They had reached the buggy by then. "Give me a week." He reached out his hand to help her up, but she ignored it.

"Fine," she stated flatly. "Now take me home."

Three days later, he was met by his younger sister on his way out to the secret place to surprise Miriam.

"Where are you going, big brother?" Rebekah asked.

"Out," he answered curtly.

"To see Miriam?" That stopped Isaac in his tracks. He spun around.

"How did you know about that?" He asked defensively. Rebekah was 14, but sometimes Isaac swore she was his second mother. Sometimes she even caught onto things faster. This was one of those times. "You can't tell Mom and Dad about this."

"Why shouldn't I?"

"Because," he responded quickly. "If you do, they'll tell Miriam's parents and then I won't be allowed to see her anymore." Rebekah rolled her eyes.

"It's not me you have to worry about. It's all your little friends out in the fields. Everyone knows you and her have been leaving the singings together every Sunday night. Besides, it's not like his forbidding you to see her has actually stopped you. So where do you go?" She almost became a detective in that moment, and Isaac thought for sure she would pull the answer out of his eyes. As if to make sure, he looked away.

"It wouldn't be a secret place if I told you," he stated. He looked at his little sister, and in that moment, he was proud of the woman she was growing up to be. Whoever the man was that would have the honor of marrying her would be the luckiest man on the planet.

"Please, don't tell Mom and Dad. I'll tell them when the time is right."

"And when is that gonna be?" She crossed her arms as if she'd just made the best argument all day. *Wow, she is sharp,* he thought.

"Soon, I promise. I have to talk to her parents first."

"Well you better do it fast or else one of the guys in the field might let it slip. Mr. Hershberger is said to be making his rounds any day now to check on his affairs. I just worry about you, Isaac. That's all." She uncrossed her arms as her face softened. "Please don't do anything you'll regret."

Isaac smiled at her. "I promise, little sister. Thank you." He gave her a hug before heading out the door. Tonight was the night, he had decided. He would ask Miriam for forgiveness for the other night. Then he would ask if they could, in fact, go steady. Not only that, he was going to talk to Mr. Hershberger if she said yes. He felt as if he couldn't get his horse to go fast enough toward the secret spot. Sometimes the old beast had a mind of his own. As soon as he was within a shorter walking distance, he got out of the buggy and began coaxing the horse through the grass into the woods before tying it hurriedly on a tree and rushing to their spot. He had a few preparations he wanted to make before she arrived, since they had agreed on meeting at sundown after Miriam put her younger siblings to bed. He had his grandmother's wedding ring on a chain around his neck that his mother had given him on the night he turned 16.

"When you find the one you want to marry, give this to her as a token of your love," Isaac's mother had said. "Explain to her what this symbolizes, and above all, don't let her go."

These thoughts were running through his head as he walked quickly toward the clearing. As he got closer however, he heard voices. Two of them to be exact: one male, and one female. His heart started racing. Who else could know about this place? Of all the years he and his friends had been coming, not one other living human being had ever been here. He decided to hide behind one of the bushes just outside of the clearing, as he couldn't see into it because of the way he and his friends had designed it over the years. He listened intently, hoping he'd be able to recognize a voice.

His heart felt as if it dropped into his stomach and he felt all color drain from his face. He recognized both voices, and they were none other than his best friends', Miriam's and Joshua's. And they sounded happy. In a panic, Isaac forgot about stealth and all of the things he had been planning for that night as he rushed out from behind his hiding place and burst into the clearing, startling his friends.

"Isaac!" Miriam exclaimed, jumping up from her seat. "I didn't expect you tonight!"

"Didn't expect me?" He suddenly couldn't think clearly. All of the words and thoughts in his head were suddenly very jumbled. *What was going on here?* He wondered. If this is what jealousy felt like, he suddenly understood why Joseph's 10 brothers threw him into an empty cistern in the book of Genesis. "How could you not expect me? We've been meeting here almost every night for the past three weeks! I told you I had something special I wanted to tell you, and you *promised* that you would be here, alone!" Isaac's voice had reached a pitch he didn't even know existed, not to mention the volume it had gone up to. He ran his hands through his hair as he began pacing around the small clearing. He tried to get his heart rate and voice back down to a level that wouldn't arouse suspicion from anyone close by. Joshua, who had been struck mute until then, finally stood up.

"Look, we didn't mean anything by it. We were just hanging out. You can still have your time—"

"How long has this been going on?" Isaac addressed Miriam, interrupting and ignoring Joshua. His voice had now become almost calm. "Is this because of what happened the other night?"

"What?" She asked. Her eyes widened, suddenly remembering. "Oh... no!"

Joshua sighed, exasperated. "Isaac," he began. "I've tried to tell you from the start. It's about getting to know her *father.* He's the one whose heart you really have to win. He doesn't want some guy he barely knows to marry his daughter."

"Some guy he barely knows?" Isaac practically roared, forgetting all pretenses of trying to keep quiet. "I grew up with her, the same as you! We've been over to her house multiple times and had the *same* conversations with him."

Miriam attempted to be the peacemaker. "Guys, please—"

"Oh, have we now?" Joshua shouted at Isaac. "So you know what Miriam is struggling with right now? That she's still in shock from your kiss the other night? The one that *you* initiated? You know that her mother is sick and she simply can't bank on someone whose heart is set on 'traveling the world' to help take care of her. How could you be so selfish?"

Those last words struck Isaac to the heart. He looked at Miriam pleading, hoping that Joshua was wrong and that all of this was just a bad dream. Had she really been putting on a pretense all for him? "Miriam? Is what he's saying true?"

Miriam stuttered but seemed to be without many words. She looked scared, but she finally nodded.

"Well Army-man," Joshua said smugly as he folded his arms. "Looks like you didn't know her as well as you thought. Maybe you should just forget this ever happened and run on home to your little fantasy land." Just then, there was the sound of men rushing in their direction. *So much for not drawing attention,* Isaac thought, mentally kicking himself for letting his emotions get so out of control. He turned to Miriam.

"Come with me."

For the third time that night, Miriam stuttered.

"Miriam, I love you. I don't know if I could go on living without you. You mean more to me than the whole world, and there's nothing I wouldn't do for you." He moved toward her, but Joshua got between them.

"Stay away from her," he warned, his eyes bright with jealousy and hurt. The voices were getting closer.

Finally Miriam spoke a clear thought. "At one point in time, I may have loved you, but I don't know if I can love a man that can't even stand up and fight for what he thinks is right... unless it's at the end of a gun."

So this whole ordeal wasn't even about the kiss. It was about Isaac's obsession with war. Most people would've taken this as a cue to change, but Isaac took it differently.

"I'll come back for you." He looked into Miriam's eyes one more time. Those beautiful green eyes. "Then you'll know that I really do love you." She furrowed her brow in confusion.

"What? Where are you going?"

"Yeah," Joshua added, also confused. "Where *are* you going?"

The voices were almost upon them now. In a flash, he took off his grandmother's wedding ring. The thought passed through Isaac's mind that the night wasn't meant to go like this. But it was too late for that. "This is a promise, that I love you and I will come back for you. Give me three years."

"The last time you promised a certain amount of time to her, you did *nothing* to deliver on that promise," Joshua reminded him with a hint of vitriol in his voice.

"We'll see," Isaac said with what he hoped was an air of mystery in his voice. Really he was just scared of the choice he was about to make.

At that moment, the first man in the search party came through the clearing. Isaac took off running deep into the woods and farther away from everything he held dear. He thought he heard someone running after him, but Isaac was the fastest man in the community, even Joshua wouldn't be able to catch him.

For the first time in his life, he felt like he was making simultaneously the best and worst decision of his life.

And it was already killing him.

"Sgt. Yoder!"

For the first time in his life, Isaac was less than excited to have those two words in the same sentence.

"Yes sir!" He addressed his commanding officer with as much respect as he could muster. Staff Sgt. Queener was his least favorite person as of late. Ever since they had gotten into a firefight with the Islamists in Iraq a few weeks prior to returning, he would find everything wrong with anything Isaac did. Queener blamed Isaac for the fact that they had gotten into the fight in the first place, and although Isaac didn't claim Queener was wrong, he also wasn't about to take responsibility.

It was our last sweep of the town, Isaac had written down in the report. War wouldn't have been so bad if there wasn't so much red tape afterward. *We were on our way back to base when a little girl came running up to me. About 10 of us were on foot to make sure if there were any civilians, we wouldn't scare them with our big vehicles. The little girl couldn't have been more than 5 or 6, and she began speaking Farsi much faster than I could translate. I asked her to slow down, but asking her seemed to have the opposite effect. At this point, the convoy had stopped, and Cpl. Lanning had begun trying to coax me that we needed to get moving. As long as the convoy was stuck, we were practically sitting ducks.*

No sooner had he said that then shots rang out from the nearest building and instantly the little girl who had just been standing in front of me suddenly had a chest full of bullets.

At this point, Isaac had had the hardest time finishing the debrief. He couldn't understand how anyone could allow someone to die like that and continue to live a normal life. One of the psychiatrists he had talked to after coming back had said Isaac would have to find a new normal, but Isaac didn't even know what normal was since he'd left his Plain ways behind to join the Army. He did know that he was responsible for that little girl's death... as well as the death of his best friend.

Instantly a firefight broke out in that little town, but all I could do was take cover. I was the group translator, so my number one priority was to stay alive at all costs. However, I also happened to be a sharp-shooter because of my upbringing, so I managed to take a few terrorists out without anyone realizing who or what hit them.

Taking the lives of those men was nothing compared to the loss of that little girl, or my best friend, Cpl. Lanning. It wasn't until the smoke had cleared that we realized we had lost him within the first few seconds of the fight. One of those first shots had been toward him, and it was a direct hit.

Lanning's life and that little girl's were what got him, not any of the terrorists' or anyone else that might have died as a result of Isaac's actions. He still had nightmares about that day. He ran through scenarios every second of the day in the back of his mind. He remembered seeing how scared the little girl was and desperately trying to decypher what she was saying. He remembered hearing the rushed tone in his best friend's voice and—after thinking about it every night for the past month—he realized he even remembered Cpl. Lanning's last words before getting shot in the throat.

"Come on man, don't do something you'll regret."

It wouldn't have been so chilling if it wasn't so close to the last thing he had heard his sister Rebekah say to him almost 3 years ago.

"I said, did you hear me, Sergeant!?"

Queener's voice snapped him back to the present.

"Yes, sir!"

"This is a disgrace! How could you just put in a request like this? You're one of my best men!"

Maybe Isaac would've listened if he hadn't already had this conversation with himself in his head. Every decision he'd made in the past two and a half years, he'd made after deciding if hearing Staff Sgt. Queener's voice was worth it.

In this case, it was because the request that Queener was so upset about was a request to leave the Army. He needed a signature and recommendation from his commanding officer before he could get out. His time wasn't up, but it had been almost three years, and he had promised Miriam Hershberger three years. He wasn't about to renege on his promise, even if he wasn't even sure she had really waited for him.

In the middle of Queener's rant, he finally said, "I have to go see about a girl, sir."

That stopped Queener in his tracks. "Oh," he said stupidly, after a few moments. "Well, why didn't you say that to begin with?"

The next few weeks of paperwork went by at a turtle's pace, but finally Isaac was out and on his way back. He hadn't looked back at his Amish life in three years, except to think about Miriam everyday.

What would it look like now that he had had a taste of freedom and the English life? Would anybody recognize him? Would anybody care? Would Miriam care? Did she keep his grandmother's ring? What about Joshua? Did he tell everyone what Isaac had done, or did he just take Miriam for his own? He suddenly had an insatiable ache to see his friends and to give them the biggest hug ever and just weep on their shoulders.

"I should've stayed to fight," he had told his first and only friend in the Army, Cpl. Lanning. "I loved her, but I didn't know how to fight."

Lanning had leaned back to look at the ceiling before stating simply, "I don't know, the whole system sounds fishy to me. You were either going to win her or not, and if she didn't really love you, then what was the point of even 'giving it a try?' I don't know about you, but I think you leaving was the best decision you could make. Don't feel sorry for the fact that you may have just won her heart by becoming the most unreachable man she's ever known."

Isaac wasn't really sure where Lanning had gotten all of his wisdom from; Isaac had asked him one time what he thought about God and the Bible, but Lanning had just laughed at him.

"That stuff is for little kids and the weak at heart! You're better than that, Yoder."

Despite what Lanning said, Isaac held true to his faith. It was the only thing that got him out of bed in the mornings... especially after coming back from war without Lanning. He tried to push that out of his mind as he was getting closer to his hometown. Like a wave, he felt all of the shame and regret from three years ago wash over him. Coupled with the recent loss of the little girl and Lanning, the pain was almost unbearable.

He didn't know why, but he decided to stop at the secret spot, maybe to get the last look at his childhood memories. No matter how today turned out, Isaac decided, he was leaving at sundown, with or without Miriam. Not surprisingly, the clearing was empty. It was the middle of the workday, so Isaac was pretty sure it would've been void of life.

Walking into town was going to be the hardest part, Isaac had decided. Because he left, and without saying goodbye to anyone but Miriam and Joshua, he was sure a lot of people would be upset about him leaving. There weren't a lot of people at the shops because they were all in the fields or in the nearest English town working. Out of habit and homesickness, Isaac went to his parents' shop. Before his eyes had even adjusted to the dimness of the store, he was tackled by the biggest hug he had ever received.

"OH, Isaac!" It was Rebekah. Instantly, Isaac returned the hug and they just held each other and wept. Finally Isaac broke the hug.

"Where's Mom and Dad?" He asked. Rebekah looked down and began crying again.

"They're gone, Isaac." She looked back up at him. "The pain of you leaving was too much to bear. Mom passed away within a month, and Dad just passed last week.

That wave of shame and guilt suddenly felt like a tsunami of emotions. He needed to sit down. Rebekah must have noticed the color drain from his face, because she quickly pulled him to the nearest chair and began fanning him.

"I'm sorry, Isaac," she finally whispered. "I tried to find out where you were to tell you, but you made yourself almost impossible to find."

"No," Isaac finally forced out. "I'm sorry... for leaving you alone like this." He looked up at her quickly. An idea was forming in his head. "Come with me."

Rebekah was shocked. "What? Come with you? You're not coming back?"

Isaac shook his head. "I came back to get Miriam, no matter what it takes."

Rebekah looked away as her face flushed.

"What?" Isaac prodded. "Tell me."

"Well," Rebekah seemed to struggle with the right words. "She's supposed to get married tomorrow... to Joshua Hostetler."

All feelings of guilt suddenly left as adrenaline kicked in. He stood up quickly. "Little sister, I need your help."

Rebekah looked unsure, but nodded. "Okay," she said. "I'll go with you too."

Isaac was actually taken back by that. "Really?"

"Yeah, it's not like any of the available guys are all that interesting here anyway. What else is there? This shop?" She laughed sadly. Isaac moved over to her.

"Hey," he cooed as he enveloped her in his arms again. "It's alright. If you don't want to leave, I understand."

"It's not that I don't want to leave," she admitted. "It's that I don't want to forget about my parents."

Isaac pulled Rebekah back and looked into her face. "Hey. As long as we're alive, our parents will never be forgotten. We keep their memories alive by the way we live."

"But would our parents want us to just leave our community like this?"

"The better question would be, do our parents want us to be miserable in this community?"

Rebekah seemed to realize that Isaac had a point. Their parents had always been huge proponents of their children doing whatever they wanted, as long as they were happy and followed the Lord.

"Following the Lord is a lot easier out there than it is in here," Isaac added almost as an afterthought.

Rebekah furrowed her brow in suspicion. "Okay, Mr. Mind-reader. I don't need another Mother in my life."

They laughed. Isaac didn't realize how much Rebekah's laugh really did calm his nerves.

"Okay," he said, more seriously. "We need a plan to get to Miriam."

"I have an idea, but it requires a lot from you."

Nothing could be worse than the rest of my life without Miriam in it, Isaac thought as Rebekah began laying out her plan.

It was finally here. The moment Miriam had been raised and trained for all her life. Her parents were so excited, but she couldn't help feeling just a little empty. It must have shown in her face because her mother brought it up.

"Honey, what's wrong?" Ruth asked. "Today should be the happiest day of your life, but you look like your favorite doll just got stolen."

"Mama, it's just not the same without Isaac here. He was one of my best friends too, and it's hard knowing that he can't be here to see this."

"I know, honey," her mother said sympathetically. "But it might just be better this way. You know Daddy never liked Isaac much anyway."

Miriam sighed heavily. That didn't make it any better, but she had to give credit to Ruth for trying. She wasn't supposed to get married until later that evening, because there were a lot of preparations going into this day. She wouldn't even be in her dress until midday, when they would start preparing her makeup and hair for the ceremony later on.

"You look beautiful," a familiar voice said. Miriam spun around to see who it was, half hoping it was Isaac Yoder, since she had just dreamed last night that he had rode into town on a horse and swept her away from this whole world. It was her father, Jacob, and he looked the proudest she had ever seen him. She smiled wide.

"Thank you, Daddy," she curtsied playfully as he moved into the room to give her a hug.

"I'm so proud of you, Miriam Joy," his voice sounded husky, like he was holding back tears. "So proud."

She pulled back a little bit to look into his face. It occurred to her that this was the beginning of a new era for her father, since she was the first of five girls that would be getting married over the course of the next ten years.

"I'm just glad Mama gets to be here to see this," Miriam said thankfully.

"Mmm," was all Jacob could force out, as tears were now flowing freely. He kissed his eldest daughter on the head and left the room. Miriam wasn't sure how she would feel if Isaac did show up today, but after seeing her father cry, she didn't know if she'd be able to bring herself to leave him like Isaac seemed to do with so much ease three years ago. He had made it look so easy, but she could hardly bear the thought of leaving her family alone for one minute.

Or so she hoped.

That hope is what Isaac and Rebekah were doing their best to play on. Rebekah hadn't become extremely close to Miriam over the past few years, but she knew enough to know that Miriam would most likely leave with Isaac if he showed up and asked her to. True to Lanning's prediction, Miriam had grown more fond of Isaac... even to the point of intentionally waiting exactly three years to get married.

Isaac saw it as a test of his love; would he be willing to potentially ruin his best friends' wedding if it meant winning the love of his life? Without a thought, Isaac knew the answer was yes. He had made too many mistakes in his life to let this one try to rule him.

Rebekah told Isaac that Miriam would be going to the flower shop alone right before heading back to her house to get dressed for the wedding. That would be the best time to talk to her.

True to predictions, Miriam walked into the flower shop alone. Isaac made no time at all in getting there. He was destined to do this long before the wedding.

"Miriam Hershberger," he declared before his eyes had adjusted from the sun outside to the darker interior. By the time they had, he realized he was standing face to face with none other than Miriam.

In another lifetime, he might have taken a step back and apologized for standing so close to her. This was not another lifetime. For the first time in three years, Isaac smelled that sweetness emanating off of her. She had pulled herself so close to him just like that night in the secret spot, but this time Isaac made the move. He pulled her in tight and kissed her fully on the lips. It was like fire and ice, burning and refreshing all at the same time.

It was just like Miriam's dream! Not only had Isaac returned, but he was there to take her away. This kiss confirmed it. She pulled herself as close as she could to him, determined to never let him go. Finally, he pulled himself away, drinking in every detail of her with his eyes.

"Come away with me."

"What about Joshua? And my father?"

Isaac was undaunted. "What about them? Are you living your life for them... or for yourself?" His voice was barely a whisper, but to Miriam it seemed as if he was shouting. He was shouting, *I love you! I desire you! Come away with me! Never look back!*

"Do you know what day it is?" Miriam asked him. He smiled.

"May 28th. Three years to the day that I told you I would be back. You waited for me."

"I knew you would come." She pulled the ring off from around her neck. "This is for you; it's a symbol of my undying love and devotion to you. I don't know why I ever treated you the way I did, Isaac. I—"

He put his finger on her lips. "Whatever happened in the past is in the past. Now is the only moment worth living for." He looked deep into her eyes. "Will you come with me right now?"

"Yes!" There wasn't a second thought in Miriam's mind. She didn't care what anyone thought or what would happen to her. She was in the arms of the man she had always truly loved.

Getting Miriam to leave without saying goodbye to anyone was the hardest thing to do, so Isaac compromised. They both went to see Joshua.

Joshua was at the church getting preparations ready. Normally he wouldn't be doing anything, but he wanted to surprise her. Then he turned around and saw what seemed like two ghosts coming down the aisle toward him. As soon as Joshua saw them coming, he knew that his life with Miriam was over. He had finally been bested by his best friend, Isaac Yoder. They not only looked happy, but also like they were about to leave.

"You're leaving with my girl?" Joshua said with a twinge of hurt in his voice.

"Come with us, Joshua," Miriam pleaded. Joshua only shook his head.

"A love triangle might sell in the world of books, but it doesn't work in real life." Joshua put his hand out toward Isaac. Isaac took it. "You bested me, old friend. Now don't mess it up."

Isaac smiled. He could tell by the way Joshua responded that even he saw this coming. "Thank you, old friend. I do wish you would come with us, but you're right about the whole love triangle. Besides, I think Rachel Swartz still likes you." Isaac winked. Joshua only smiled.

"Get out of here before I change my mind. Besides, you can't just take the whole community with you. There would be no one to make awesome tourist attractions to intrigue soldiers coming back from war."

Isaac had to laugh at Joshua's attempt to be funny. He was taking this better than Isaac expected, and that was all that really mattered in that moment.

"Goodbye, Joshua Hostetler."

"Goodbye, Isaac Yoder. Don't get too crazy out there. Goodbye, Miriam. I hope your life is all of the happiness you're wishing for and more. You deserve it."

Miriam smiled. "Thank you so much." She went to hug Joshua, but he pulled away.

"Don't make this any harder than it already is," he warned. Now Isaac could see that he really was hurt. It broke his heart that it had to end like this, but he was glad that Miriam would be with him.

"I'll write to you from time to time," Isaac said. "The Hardy Brothers need some new adventures anyway."

They shared a moment of camaraderie before Isaac and Miriam turned and walked out of the church and into their new lives.

They met Rebekah at the secret place. "I talked to your dad," she addressed Miriam. "He cried. He wanted me to give you this. I guess he always knew this was coming." She pulled out a small book: her grandmother's diary. She had never been allowed to open it, but she had been told stories from it.

"I guess he was going to give it to you at the wedding, but since he'll never see you again..." Rebekah trailed off.

There were a few moments of no talking before Isaac finally said, "Let's go. It's time to start our new life together."

He smiled as he put his arms around his sister and his lifelong love. As bittersweet as the parting was, it was the best decision he had ever made. In that moment, there was nowhere else he'd rather be than in the arms of the woman he loved.

BENEATH THE AMISH SKY

NIKKI SALEM

<u>Chapter One</u>

She didn't love him.

She'd never love him.

Anna knew better than to think in absolutes, knew that she shouldn't assume she knew better than her father, but she would never love Samuel. Not if she was given a thousand years, not if he were actually closer to her age.

She was hardly twenty-one.

Hardly out of age for going to Sings and getting to court properly, her Rumspringa wasn't even finished.

Her father thought he knew what was best for her.

Samuel was an absolute nightmare though.

He was almost thirty-five, married once but his wife left to be English.

When Anna had first heard about this she felt terrible for him. It was horrifying to think that someone you pledged your life to could just leave you behind without a second thought. To live a life neither of you were familiar with. Anna couldn't imagine how selfish and cruel his ex-wife must have been. Leaving behind a chance at growing a family, at starting a life together, sounded outrageous-

Until she properly got to know Samuel.

His wife had made the right decision, and as she knew him better Anna began to envy the mystery woman who had flown the coup.

Samuel was boring, uninteresting, repetitive. He worked in the church, which her father found more than respectable, and so all he spoke of was the church. He went on for literal hours about repairs he wanted to do to the meeting building, hardly pausing to breathe. He didn't care to listen to her, or to stop once she was obviously uncomfortable. In all of the hours her parents had let him speak with her, she'd probably spoken less than twenty words.

She didn't want to have to live with that forever.

Anna couldn't imagine another sixty years, or more, of her life dedicated to this man who didn't care about anything but himself and the image the church gave him.

She couldn't see herself ever loving him, so marriage was a horrifying prospect.

The evening sun was just beginning to settle on the edge of the horizon. Her father had made up his mind, and all she could do was hope to dissuade him somehow. Gathering the last of the laundry for the next day, she listened for his tell-tale footsteps.

He was her father, she knew it was sad to be so nervous, but she was.

Sucking in a deep breath, she urged her feet forward, out to the kitchen where he was standing and drinking water.

"Father, may we speak?" she asked, her hands settled in front of her.

"Yes, what is it?" he asked, he was covered in mud from the day's work.

"I can't marry Samuel," she laid the words out neatly between them. Her father's mood seemed to immediately crumple into aggravation.

"You will," he replied back simply.

"Father I don't love him," she said, shaking her head. "He's so boring, I can't imagine a worse match," she admitted, approaching him.

"What does that matter?" her father asked, his voice raising. "You're supposed to be building a home and a family together, you'll love him in the end," he shook his head.

"I won't marry him," she said, standing her ground in a way she never had with her father.

"Are you saying my decisions aren't good enough for you?" he asked, slamming his hat down on the table.

"No, I-"

"You are my daughter, you had your chance to choose, that's over," he said sternly.

"I can still choose to leave," she said, hoping the words would bite him so he'd realize what he was saying. His face dropped into one of dark anger.

"If you will not listen to me, you *can* leave," his voice was like the grave, and it stung her.

"Father-"

"I will not have you speaking out against me, I make the decisions, I would rather have you married with him than unmarried with nothing but a dream of romance," her father was red faced in anger.

"Then I'll leave!" she shot back, the words slipped past her lips before she could catch them.

The air between them was still and quiet.

The moment stretched thinly, until a cough in the next room let Anna know her mother was nearby. She had a habit of listening in on conversations, and Anna couldn't hold it against her.

"I'll be gone by tomorrow night," Anna added, the words terrifying and unreal feeling even as she said them.

***

She didn't sleep that night.

Anna spent the night shoving what she could into a couple bags. Her clothing was plain, but plenty. She wasn't sure what she was planning on doing, on where she was planning on going. She just knew that if she spent another night under the same roof as her father she was going to explode.

Samuel wasn't an option.

In the blue light of morning she heard her father leave for his work.

Out her window she watched him pause for a moment, looking towards her window, and then step up onto his buggy and leave.

Just as well, she reminded herself, it would be easier to leave if he wasn't there.

As she started to drag her two bags to the front, her mother stopped her.

"Anna," her mother said, soothing a hand over Anna's right arm. "Are you sure you want to do this?" she asked softly.

"No," Anna admitted. "The only thing I'm sure I want in this world is that I do not want to be with Samuel," she explained.

"You could stay, reason with him, be patient with your father," her mother said gently.

"You know better than I do that's not an option," Anna sighed. "It's easier this way, otherwise I know I'd end up marrying Samuel," she explained.

"Alright," her mother replied. "You should take this though," she added, handing a small envelope to Anna. "It'll get you through long enough until you get a job," she tucked her arms tight around Anna. "You can always come back to me, my Anna, your father is stubborn but he'll miss you," she explained.

"He'll not want me back after this," Anna argued, feeling tears prickle at her eyes.

"You're his daughter, he always will have a spot for you," she countered,

"Thank you, mother," Anna sobbed, rubbing her eyes as the tears free fell.

"Of course my daughter," her mother answered, hugging her again. "I love you very much, I'll do anything for you to be happy," she added.

When her mother set to starting to clean laundry for the day, Anna was forced to start her journey.

The world looked too ordinary, too regular, for what day it was.

She steeled herself, and started her walk out of the village she'd always lived in. Out to where she knew cars would take her to a city, to a place so impossibly different and strange to her.

Anything was better than Samuel, though.

Chapter Two

Within her first week she'd already gone through over half of the three thousand her mother left her.

Anna was an intelligent girl, though. She'd found a room to rent in a Victorian home, something not too unfamiliar from what homes she was used to, for just a couple hundred a month. She paid six months of it in advance, and spent the rest on clothes, food, and a phone, to make herself to fit in.

Her new landlady, Holly, was to thank for most of the ideas and shopping.

She was a forty year old woman, and so kind, Anna was thankful she'd found her listing in the news paper. Not everything was as unfamiliar as she'd imagined.

People treated her differently, but as long as she ignored them they'd have nothing to say.

A couple men had talked to her, shown interest in her, but she had ignored all of them. She was sure she was being rude, she was sure that she'd never make any friends this way, but she also was sure that friendship wasn't what these men were wanting.

She'd never date.

Never go after any men, or marry.

She'd decided this on the ride out from her home.

Anna knew that she'd never find a man, an English man, who her parents would approve of. She couldn't marry someone they didn't approve of, even if she wasn't a part of the church anymore. In her heart she knew it would be the wrong thing to do.

She loved the idea of love, of finding someone who you match with perfectly, but she couldn't feel right being in that kind of love if it meant her family would look down on her for it.

She already had enough shame to bear.

The only thing left to do was to find a job.

Holly had gathered a list of places for Anna to look. Everything ranging from lawyer's offices, to factories that made holiday chocolate all year round.

She'd bought comfortable shoes, though, and she was happy to go to each business and try to impress with what she could. There wasn't much on her resume, but she had to try.

If not she'd have squandered her mother's money for nothing.

The general response to her from most companies was an extreme naked curiosity. They'd look at her like she grew a few extra heads during the conversation, and keep her there to talk to them for a bit. Just when she'd think she was closing the deal on the job, most places would apologize and say they were looking for someone with more experience.

She took that to mean they wanted someone who could operate a computer.

Her courage was waning, she wanted to get hired quickly, to be able to send her mother back a return of what she'd been given. Nothing was turning up, though, after a week and a half of, almost constant, searching.

Fearful for what was leftover of the money, not wanting to let herself have too much access to it, Anna found herself inside a bank.

The building was cold, refreshing against the summer sun, and empty besides her and a teller behind one of the long counters.

He caught her eyes, and a curdling guild set low in her stomach immediately.

He was gorgeous.

This stranger, with a name tag that shimmered out Andre, held her attention with more strength than Samuel had in any of the time she'd known him. His curly brown hair was combed back away from strong cheekbones and glittering green eyes. His shoulders looked broad, strong, and he seemed taller than most men she'd seen in the city.

When he looked up back at her, Anna felt chills run through her, and her face heated.

She didn't need to think about that, though, she was on a mission.

"Good afternoon," he greeted, setting aside the papers he was looking at. His voice was deep, echoing in the empty bank.

"Good afternoon," she mirrored. "I was hoping to open an account," she said, unsure how to phrase this. She regretted not asking Holly for help on this.

"I can help you with that," he smiled, turning to his computer. "Checking or savings?" he asked, typing.

"Checking, please," she responded, letting her eyes fall on his hands for just a moment before she looked away.

"Do you have two kinds of identification?" he asked, his typing stopped.

"Yes," she answered, pulling out the state ID she'd gotten just in the last week, and her birth certificate.

He accepted them and then froze.

"Are you Amish?" he asked, he looked stunned. "Or- were- you Amish?" he corrected himself, something nobody else had done.

"I was," she agreed. Her birth certificate named the only Amish town within a hundred miles.

"I was as well," he said, his eyes shining with nostalgia.

"You were?" she said, surprised for once.

"Yes, I was with a town in Idaho, I've been out of the church for five years," he answered.

"I just left the church almost two weeks ago," Anna said meekly.

"Well, welcome to the madness," he replied, a joke in his voice. She immediately felt comfortable with him.

This had never happened to her before.

"Thank you," she answered, unsure of the proper reply.

"I'll go ahead and set up your account," he started typing her information into the computer. "Will you want to use direct deposit for your job?" he asked, handing back her documents.

"I don't have a job yet," she admitted, embarrassed.

He typed something, and then paused for a moment.

"Have you applied here?" he asked.

"No," she answered, embarrassed at herself for overlooking the opportunity.

"We've been holding walk-in interviews, I can get the manager over to talk with you, if you'd like," he offered. "They're very happy to train, here," he said.

"That would be amazing," Anna said, surprised at her own luck.

As she watched him walk away, she could feel herself getting quickly attached. She knew she'd promised herself she'd stay away from boys.

She'd sworn she wouldn't date.

Still, she felt an attraction, an interest in him, that she'd never felt with anyone else. If she was going to live an English life, she owed herself to at least properly try it.

***

The interview was simple.

An older man, older than her father, asked her a handful of questions about her life an experience. He didn't seem phased that she'd never touched a computer until the last couple of weeks.

She stood up as the interview ended, expecting him to say they were looking for someone with more experience.

"Would you be available to start training tomorrow?" he asked instead, opening the door into for her.

"Yes!"

Chapter Three

Working with Andre was testing her convictions.

He was placed in charge of training her, helping her figure out the computers and the cash counting machines. Andre was patient, kind, and took his time with her even when customers were around.

She learned he'd moved into the state right after he left the church. He didn't own a television, but watched shows on a computer he had a home. She learned he liked to order lunch in, but always forgot to eat breakfast.

She learned he was incredibly generous with his smiles.

Regardless of how simple, how quick, her attachment to him had been within the first couple minutes of meeting him, it had grown into something stronger.

They bonded over talking about similar life experiences, over finding out what differences set them apart. He'd ridden in cars a lot growing up, none owned by his family, while she'd never been in a computer until the last couple weeks.

He was like a piece of her home that she'd left behind.

A warm blanket in the starkness of the new world she was getting used to.

A couple weeks into working together he asked her to dinner, and she couldn't make herself say no.

He picked a place close to her home, and she was both thrilled and terrified.

Holly immediately took the helm.

"I haven't dated in ten years, but you make me feel like I'm the one going out to night," Holly laughed, helping her pick out something to wear. "It's so funny that you're both Amish, isn't it?" she asked, Anna couldn't see the humor, but she nodded anyways.

"I think blue is really the best color for you," Holly said, pulling back Anna's hair so that it didn't cover the simple dress too much.

"Thank you," Anna said.

"But- are you sure you don't want to wear something brighter? Something turquoise and bright would really catch his eye," Holly offered, looking her over.

"No, for him I'd prefer to be myself," Anna smiled.

"Mm, alright," Holly tapped her shoulder, and Anna leaned her head back to let her braid her hair. They'd grown close very quickly, and Anna was glad to have someone in her corner. "He may be Amish, but he's still a boy, if you need anything please call me," Holly said, pausing to look Anna over in the mirror again. "You're gonna knock his socks off," she added, smiling.

***

The restaurant was busy when Anna arrived. She was early, so she requested a table, and then sat there and stared at the crowd.

She couldn't imagine what kinds of lives everyone in that building led. Jobs she'd probably never heard of, homes and cars that would blow her mind, problems she couldn't fathom. She couldn't imagine growing up in a world like this.

Anna listened to small snippets of conversations, catching foreign sounding ideas and words, until Andre arrived.

She was the one blown away.

He looked like he'd stepped out of a magazine. She was suddenly stunned to remember that he'd started out like her.

He'd integrated so well into this world that nobody around them would ever guess that he was Amish.

With her, she was sure people would figure it out.

He was amazing.

"Sorry I'm a little late, my Uber got lost," he apologized, sitting across from her.

"It's fine," she shook her head, smiling. She wasn't quite sure what an Uber was, but she told herself she'd ask him later.

The beginning of the date was jittery, she was nervous, and he seemed to be able to tell. She wanted to make a good impression, but was terrified that trying too hard would make her look like she'd forgotten her parents and church.

By the time they finished eating, though, she'd calmed down.

"Why did you leave the church, if I can ask," he said, stacking their plates he slid them to the end of the table.

"Oh, um," Anna wasn't sure how to explain it. She couldn't say she refused marriage, it would look like she'd never wanted to date anyone ever, but she knew she really wanted to date Andre. "My father and I had a disagreement, and he told me to leave," she explained, feeling shame at the explanation.

"Oh, I'm sorry," he said sincerely.

"It's fine," she lied. "I'm enjoying seeing what life out here is like," she admitted.

"I'm glad you're having a good time," he smiled. "So you'd rather be out here?" he asked.

"I'm not sure about that," she shook her head. "I just couldn't stay there," she tried to explain.

"Ah, I completely understand that," he agreed, take one last sip of his water.

"What about you? Why are you out here?" she asked.

"Mm, same thing, disagreements," he said. Anna wondered, her heart in her stomach, if he'd had a similar experience to her. She tried to picture him being forced into marriage, and the idea made her ache for him.

She was glad that his experiences led to him being in front of her, but was upset that it meant he had to be away from his family and the church.

"I want to go back, though," he admitted.

"Really?" Anna was surprised.

"Yes, of course, maybe not the same town, or the same people, but I miss the church. There's no sense of community or wholeness out here, I miss that so much it hurts," he explained.

"Oh," she said, surprised by him again.

She hadn't considered going back.

She'd only been gone a couple of weeks, and although she missed her family and connections she still felt better out in the world than stuck being married to Samuel. If he wanted to go back then her flirting with him was pointless. She wouldn't return with him and risk her father being disappointed in her.

Anna confirmed with herself that she was better off when she had sworn off dating.

When she finally decided this, looking back up at Andre he seemed concerned.

"What's wrong?" he asked, setting down his drink.

"Oh, nothing, I was just thinking about home," she lied.

"I get that," he nodded, continuing to eat.

She's have to stop seeing him.

Have to stop talking to him outside of professionally.

If he fell for her she'd end up hurting him and disappointing her family.

Anna continued to eat as she berated herself. If she was more thoughtful, more intelligent, she would have saved everyone a lot of heartache.

She'd tasted human interaction and became a glutton for it.

Chapter Four

It was harder to ignore Andre than she thought.

First of all, they worked together on every shift- which meant that he'd be within ten feet of her for most of an eight hour shift. Within the first half hour of their first shift together the following Monday he seemed to notice something had changed.

At first he spared her the embarrassment of asking her why.

They worked silently together, he helped her if she needed it, but kept his tone formal and plain. She did the same even though it hurt.

She wasn't sure why it hurt so much.

Anna hadn't known him for even a month, but looking at him and knowing she couldn't talk to him comfortably- knowing she couldn't hold his eye contact- anymore hurt her.

The first week of working together like this was like torture for her. He was a cold drink that her parched throat could never have. Their boss told them that their productivity was up and they had been doing a great job, and it was almost embarrassing. Had she been so distracted that she didn't work her best when she was talking to him?

Had she let him steal away her mind that much?

Anna was sure that the worst had passed. She was sure that he'd let go of his feelings for her, and she of hers, and that they could move on as regular coworkers. It wasn't something she was sure she wanted, and it hurt, but she told herself that it was for the best.

On the next Monday when she went in, someone was in Andre's spot besides him.

It was Kat, from the weekend, and some evening, shifts.

"Where's Andre?" Anna asked, trying to keep herself from seeming invested in the answer.

"He's out sick," Kat said, filling her drawer for the morning rush. "He called in last night," she added.

Anna's heart ached.

"What's wrong with him?" she asked.

"A flu probably," Kat guessed, shrugging. "Can you get me a couple more pens for my station before you get back here?" she asked.

"Yes, of course," Anna said, walking to the storage area.

He was sick.

He was sick and she didn't know? Her own stomach was turning and aching in fear. If she was over him why did it scare her so much just to hear he had the flu?

Why would she care so deeply?

Anna grabbed the pens and headed out.

She'd visit him after her shift.

***

Anna shouldn't have been able to get his home address.

She could have called him ahead and asked for it, but instead she asked Kat for help. If she called him her resolve would break. Anna just wanted to bring him some food and make sure he was okay. She wasn't going to stay long, she wasn't going to let herself say more than twenty words.

That's all.

She stood in front of his apartment complex, staring down the front of it like she was looking for answers.

Why did she care so much?

Why was a bag of hot soup and bread in her hand, why was she standing in front of a random man's home instead at her own home eating her own dinner? Why did it matter if he was okay?

At first she tried to convince herself that it was because he was Amish too, and that she was seeking that familial connection the entire Amish community shares. She knew that wasn't true. She knew better than to lie to herself.

Anna buzzed his room's number from the dial pad, and waited patiently.

"Hello?" he sounded sleepy and her heart warmed.

"I heard you were sick, I've brought food," eight words, she counted as she spoke them.

"I'll be right down," his voice chirped out quickly, like he was surprised. Anna was relieved he hadn't asked her to come up to him instead, she didn't want to appear to be straying any further from her convictions than she had.

"Hey," he said, opening the door after a minute. He looked ruffled, his hair askew and his shirt wrinkled. Her heart warmed at the sight of him, even when he was sick he was still handsome.

"Hi," nine words. She begged for her voice not to betray her.

"Come in, just to the lobby," he said gently, opening the door further. Anna knew she shouldn't but she did anyways.

"How are you feeling?" thirteen words. She could only allow herself seven more. If she went any further she didn't trust herself.

"A lot better," he said, fixing his hair with his hands. "I slept it off most of the day, drank a lot of tea and had a hot bath," he explained. "I should be back at work tomorrow," he added.

"That's good to hear," three words left.

"Yeah," he answered. Then paused for a moment and looked her seriously in the eyes. Anna felt like he was staring right into her mind. "How are you? You've been- different- this last week," he said. Anna considered her words carefully.

"I've been fine," she answered.

Twenty.

She needed to keep her mouth shut.

"Okay," he said gently. A silence hung between them, she knew he expected her to say more, she willed her mouth shut.

Anna handed him the bag of food, and then stepped back towards the door.

"Bye, then," he said, unsure.

Anna nodded, her hand on the handle to open it.

"Anna-" he said gently. She froze, not sure what to do. "Have I done something wrong? Have I hurt you in some way? If so, I'm sorry, I'll ask to be transferred to another location," he offered. "I've really enjoyed getting to know you, I'm sorry f I've made you unhappy," he continued.

Anna's hand tightened on the handle of the door as she felt her resolve start to unravel. He started to step away, and any less will power she had completely dissolved into the air.

"I can't go back and live there," she said softly, feeling tears prickle at her eyes. "I was foolish and got into a fight with my father, I refused to marry someone they wanted me to, and I ran off like a child," she explained, actually crying now. "You want to go back, and I can't give you that, I can't," she explained, shaking. "If I go back there my father won't care, he'll make me marry this stranger," she explained.

"Have you talked to him since then?" Andre asked, walking back to her. "It sounds like you both jumped into it quickly, have you talked about it?"

"I've only sent letters to my mother," Anna shook her head.

"I'm not even sure your town would accept me," Andre said gently.

"What?"

"Come sit down," he motioned to a couple chairs in the lobby. Anna nodded and wiped the tears from her eyes. She never thought she'd like him this much.

Never even considered it.

"I was forced to leave because my village was convinced that I stole something from a brother of mine, even though I was out of town when it happened," he explained. "He told them I stole and sold one of their horses to the English, and they believed him. I was made to leave within a week," he explained.

"You wouldn't do that," she gasped, disgusted someone would spread a story like that.

"No, I wouldn't," he agreed. "My brother was always greed, though, and my father just recently passed. Their house was to be mine, and now it's his," he said.

"That's awful," Anna shook her head, upset.

"It's how it is," Andre shrugged. "I won't make you go anywhere you don't want to, I won't make you do anything you don't want to, but please don't shut me out like that anymore," he said gently.

"Okay," Anna nodded, feeling drained and embarrassed.

He was too kind, too understanding.

"I want to speak to my father," she admitted.

"Want me to be there for it?" he offered.

"Maybe," she sighed, wiping the last of the moisture off her face. "You should eat," she added.

"Alright," he stood slowly, walking her to the door. "Thank you for talking to me."

"Of course," she said, feeling foolish for treating him how she did.

Andre leaned down and kissed her forehead gently, before opening the door for her. Anna could feel her heart rushing the whole walk home.

What did she want?

Chapter Five

She was in front of her home again.

Regardless of where she went, who she was in the world, this place would always be her home.

She'd waited the entire week, had pressured herself into patience as she tried to figure out what to say. She wasn't asking to marry Andre, he hadn't asked her, but she wanted to court him.

She wanted her parents to be a part of her life.

She couldn't silence how she felt about them, she couldn't hide what her mind was doing.

She just wanted them to know how she felt.

Anna plucked up her courage and knocked on the door for the first time in her life. Before this she'd always been able to just go in. Before now this was always where she lived.

It was evening, the sun starting to drip down onto the horizon as the air cooled. Long blue shadows painted the fields and homes, and in the glow she felt nostalgic. There were footsteps inside, and she waited patiently, her heart hammering in her ears.

"Anna?" her mother gasped as she opened the door. Anna was swept into her arms, pulled tight and close, and Anna could feel the shudder of her mother starting to cry. "I thought all I'd ever see of you anymore was letters," her mother sobbed out, clutching her against herself.

"No, no, I'm here," Anna answered, hugging her back. She could feel tears pricking against her own eyes. "I need to speak to father," Anna said gently.

"He has hardly spoken since you left," her mother admitted wearily.

"Then I just need him to listen," Anna replied. She felt like she'd aged years since she had been there last, even though it had been less than two months.

"Alright," her mother nodded, patting her arm and pulling Anna into the home.

The house smelled of dinner and dishes, her mother had been cleaning when Anna arrived, and it took all of her willpower not to distract herself into helping clean.

"Anna is here," her mother said as they entered the sitting room. Her father was there, the bible in his lap. When he looked up at her, his eyes seemed so sad. Her heart broke for him.

"Father," Anna said gently, moving to sit next to him on the couch. He watched her quietly, only breaking his silence to itch his beard. She could remember growing up and pulling on his beard as a young girl. He looked so old now. "I'd like to talk to you for a short while," she explained. He nodded, and glanced up at her mother, who then went back to the kitchen to continue cleaning.

"You're not wearing English clothing," he noted.

"I'm not English," she reminded him. It was good to hear his voice. "I want to apologize for going wild as I did, and not listening to you," she explained. "I don't regret not marrying Samuel, but I do regret arguing with you and disrespecting you." He was quiet as she spoke, listening to each word she said with immense consideration.

"I have met an Amish man while I've been out there, and I wish to court him," she explained simply. "I'm not here to beg you to accept him, or to tell you that I wish to marry him, I just don't want to keep any part of my life from you," she said. Her father nodded.

"Who is this man?" he asked, his voice was patient, not accusing.

"He's a coworker of mine at a bank, he's kinda and intelligent," she answered.

"He's Amish?"

"Yes, and he wants to join the church again and it will have him," she said. "I want to come home father, he wants to come with me, I miss my family and world," she explained.

Her father was quiet for a while, mulling over everything he just heard. Anna was patient and watched him carefully. Her mother walked by the outside of the room more often than was necessary, she knew she was listening for an answer as well.

Her father took her hand gently and stared down at it.

"Your mother has missed you," he said softly. She knew that he meant he did as well, she didn't question it. "When I chased you away like I did I was brash, I wasn't thinking about what was best for everyone," he explained. "I wanted you to have marriage, to have happiness, like your mother and I have found. I didn't consider that Samuel would ever make you unhappy," he continued. "I'll meet this man," he explained.

Anna reached forward and grasped her father into her arms. She hadn't hugged him in years, hadn't thought to, but she needed to hold her father. His arms wrapped around her as well, and she felt like a child again.

"I just want you to be happy," he said, his voice went weak for a moment, and she willed herself to ignore it. If her father cried, she's save him the embarrassment of knowing she'd seen it.

"I'm sorry I didn't treat you with the respect you've earned," she responded, holding him tight.

They sat there for a moment, reunited and feeling every inch of how apart they were.

"When can I meet him?" her father asked, leaning back away from her. There was a shine to her eyes that she felt her heart warm to.

"He's outside. He dressed in clothes he still had from his last town, he's waiting just outside of the fence," she admitted, bowing her head. "He requested to meet you both," she added. Her mother now stopped in the hall, no longer pretending she was carrying laundry back and forth for the tenth time. Setting down the basket, she approached the two of them and sat her hands on her husbands shoulder.

"We'll see him," her father said, nodding.

Anna nodded, and rushed out to get him.

"They want to see you," she said gently, pulling him out of his thoughts. Anxious nerves and excitement both crossed Andre's face, and she ached to wipe the lines of stress away.

"My father has forgiven me, we're okay now," she added, trying to soothe him.

"Alright," he said, taking her hand. "I love you," he added, the crickets around them were humming to life as the sun began to really set.

"I love you too," she breathed out, amazed that the words were hers, that she really meant them.

She couldn't fear anything, nothing was scary anymore.

She was in love, and her parents accepted it.

As she led him back to the house, her hand brushing against his, glad to finally be back home.

BLOSSOMING AMISH

DEE DEE ROBBINS

Chapter One

Abigail Schroder awoke to the sound of birds chirping outside of her bedroom window.

Abigail took a deep breath and let out a sad sigh. Pulling herself up in bed, she propped her back against her pillow and watched as the birds worked side-by-side to craft a home for their future family.

While she generally loved to tiptoe over to the glass and watch as the pair of happy bluebirds worked together building a nest, this morning was different. Today their merry song only brought to mind her own misery.

The birds had always reminded her of what her future life would be like. She had dreamed of a life where she and her husband would work hand-in-hand to raise up a family in their Amish community.

Now, all of Abigail's dreams had been shattered.

"Jacob," she whispered the name gently, wishing that the past two months had been

nothing more than a dream.

Jacob had been her beau since the couple had met at a young people's gathering. For the past five years they had dated.

Abigail had planned to spend her entire life by Jacob's side. She had wanted to marry him, raise children with him, and then grow old along with him.

But now it was all gone.

She had been so hopeful the night Jacob had asked to see her alone. There had been something different about him. Rather than taking her to an Amish gathering or somewhere on a date, he told her that he just wanted to talk.

After five years together, Abigail could only imagine that he was going to ask for her to marry him. She had spent the entire day with a smile on her face as she did the regular chores of hanging laundry out to dry, scrubbing the floors, and helping her two younger sisters sew new dresses.

Abigail wasn't the only one who hoped for the best. Her fourteen-year-old sister Sally had begged her to tell her what happened first, and she had noticed a spark of excitement in her parents' eyes when Jacob arrived on his buggy.

She and Jacob had laughed together as they drove out to their favorite spot on the back of his *daed's* farm. Sitting together, they watched the sun go down while butterflies danced around them.

"Abigail," Jacob had whispered as she leaned her head against his shoulder and closed her eyes, "I have something I need to tell you."

It had been different than Abigail had expected. The words sounded wrong in her ears and, rather than seeming happy, Jacob's voice sounded strained.

She had looked up at him and watched as the man she had loved for so long forced a sad smile.

"I'm leaving, Abigail." He announced the words she had never expected to hear.

"Leaving?" She had repeated, "What do you mean?"

"I'm leaving the Amish," Jacob had announced with a shrug. When he looked down at her surprise he laughed, "Come on, girl. We've been together for five years. You knew it was going to happen eventually! I don't belong here! I'm not like anyone in the community and I don't want to be."

"Jacob," Abigail had tried to change his mind, "Our future..."

"Exactly," he had interrupted, "I want a future outside of a dirty chicken farm. I want to see the world. I want to be able to drive a car and wear normal clothes. I want to be able to talk on a phone and watch television without fear of getting in trouble. I want to be free, Abigail. I want to wipe the dirt of this place and these people off my hands. I want to try being whoever Jacob wants to be!"

"What about us?" Abigail's voice had sounded like no more than a whisper.

Jacob looked down and shook his head, "Abigail...there is no more us."

That had been it. Abigail had tried to convince him to stay with the Amish community, but all she could do was cry as he drove her home.

Even now, two months later, Abigail could hardly stop the tears from rolling down her cheeks as she watched the pair of birds working together outside of her window.

"Abigail," she heard her mother's familiar voice along with a soft rap against her bedroom door, "It's time to be up. Church will begin soon. I need your help with breakfast."

"Coming, Mom," Abigail managed to call out. She scooted down in bed and closed her eyes, trying to erase all her thoughts.

Church. If there was one place that she didn't want to go, it was church. Every two weeks the Amish community gathered in a different home to perform the service that started in the morning and ended with a group meal. Growing up, Abigail had loved the Sunday ritual, but now it was one of her least favorite parts of the week.

With the loss of Jacob, it felt as if Abigail had also lost all her faith in God. She had spend the last five years of her life so sure of her future, and now it felt that it had all been ripped away from her. And now, at twenty-three-years-old, Abigail found that she was one of the oldest singles in her Amish community. It appeared that her dream to be a wife and a mother was gone for good.

It seemed God no longer had a plan or a use for Abigail Schroder.

Chapter Two

While Abigail would rather have stayed home from church, she realized that this was not an option. Although her parents had been very understanding of her heartbreak, they were unyielding where church was concerned.

"God still has a plan for you, Abigail," her *mamm* would assure her any time that Abigail would mention her lack of spiritual fervor.

So, that Sunday morning, Abigail found herself squeezed onto one of the hard wooden benches in John Yoder's house. She glanced at her sisters, Sally and Emma, who sat on either side of her. They seemed completely engrossed in the message that the preacher was providing.

"I know the plans I have for you," The preacher was reading from the Bible, "Plans to prosper you and not to harm you, plans to give you a future and a hope."

Abigail shut her eyes and tried to will herself not to cry.

God no longer had a plan for her. She knew that. All her dreams had been erased when Jacob left. Life seemed completely pointless now and the future only dark and empty.

When the preacher had finished his message, the family joined the rest of the church for a large meal out in the barn. The Yoders had provided enough food for the entire congregation with baked chicken, homemade noodles, gravy, and potatoes. While she knew the food was delicious, Abigail could hardly force herself to eat.

As she shifted her food across her plate with her fork, she thought of services past. Services when Jacob had been by her side, amusing her with his funny stories from work and making her laugh at his constant antics. How she missed him!

"Abigail," she was brought out of her thoughts when her sister Emma gave her a gentle nudge with her elbow, "Abigail, who is that man?"

Abigail looked up from her plate of food and in the direction that Emma was pointing. Sitting several tables over was a young Amish man that she didn't recognize. He was tall and thin with a shock of dark hair. Looking up, his brown eyes met Abigail's before she could look back down at her plate.

"Who is he?" Emma asked again.

Abigail shrugged her shoulders, "I have no idea."

Recently, many new couples had been moving into their community with their families.

Families...the word alone made Abigail want to cry.

She would never have a family of her own.

Looking back, she should have realized that things with Jacob had never been good. In their five years together, he had never once mentioned marriage, even while all their other friends had been tying the knot. Jacob had only ever been interested in having fun. He liked to have his own way and always got what he wanted.

The realization that Abigail had simply been someone for him to use for his enjoyment was almost more than she could stand. While she had been planning her future with him, to Jacob she was simply a stepping stone to his life apart from her.

"Pete, Lovina," She heard a voice speaking to her parents, "I have someone I want you to meet."

Abigail looked up in time to see their bishop introducing her parents to the stranger Emma had pointed out.

"This is Noah Abrams," the bishop was explaining, "He's new to the community."

Noah nodded his head and stretched out his hand to take her father's, "Mr. Schroder, it's good to meet you and your family."

Abigail's father smiled and said, "It's good to have you in the community, Noah! I'd like you to meet my wife, Lovina, and our daughters, Sally, Emma, and Abigail."

Noah nodded his head to each of the girls. It seemed to Abigail that his gaze paused on her. Staring into his dark chocolate eyes was almost more than she could bear and she had to look down at her lap.

"Oh, Abigail," Sally breathed softly as the bishop led him on to speak to someone else, "Where do you suppose his wife is? Do you think he's married? It's hard to imagine that anyone that *wunderbar gut* looking would be single!"

Abigail gave her sister a solemn glance and then continued to play with her food.

It was true, the stranger was handsome. His body was so tall and fit, his dark hair so wavy, and his eyes so incredibly deep. When he had looked at her, Abigail almost felt as if Noah Abrams could look into her very soul.

"*Ach*, Abigail," she scolded herself silently, "You better stop."

Surely looking at men was not a good idea for Abigail. When Jacob had left so had all hopes of her future; it was time she accepted that truth completely. Besides, Noah Abrams was probably married.

Chapter Three

Monday morning was the start of a new week and the day that Abigail went to go help out Mandy Eicher. Mandy was the Amish community's seamstress. Each week she took on sewing and, with her youngest daughter recently married, the workload was more than Mandy could handle on her own.

Despite the beautiful spring weather, the five-minute walk to the Eicher house left Abigail feeling morose. She wondered if this was to be the rest of her life. She wondered if each day she would do the same thing until she was an old maid.

Wiping a tear from her eye, Abigail softly whispered, "Why, Lord? What kind of life am I going to lead? If this is all you have planned for me and I am never to have the dearest wishes of my heart, why did you give me life at all?"

Abigail didn't knock on Mandy's door; instead, she simply turned the knob and stepped into the backroom where Mandy worked on the sewing.

Surprisingly enough, Mandy was not at her old fashioned sewing machine yet and the pile of laundry was still lying untouched on the table.

"Hmmm," Abigail whispered to herself, "This isn't like the Mandy that I know."

"Mandy," she called out as she started to sort through a pile of dresses, "Mandy, are ya home?"

Suddenly, the form of a little girl came scampering into the sewing room, filling the area with her giggles.

"Hi!" She greeted Abigail, a huge smile stretched across her pretty round face, "What's your name?"

Abigail raised her eyebrows in surprise. While she knew that Mandy had several grandchildren, she had never met this child before.

"I'm Abigail." Despite Abigail's sad mood, something about the little girl instantly warmed her heart.

The child pushed back a blonde curl that had escaped from her prayer cap and smiled, "Well, it's good to meet you, Abigail! My name is Katie and I'm five years old."

She seemed like such a little lady that Abigail couldn't help but smile back. She wanted to pick Katie up and give her a hug.

"You're nice," Katie announced.

"Where are your parents?" Abigail asked as she foraged through her pocket and pulled out a piece of candy to offer the child.

"Ooohhh, candy!" Katie squealed as she took the piece of peppermint, "*Danki*, Abigail! My *daed* had to go work on our new house today, so I have to stay here with Aunt Mandy."

"What about your mama?"

Katie shrugged sadly, her face suddenly clouding over, "I never had one...but I want one awful badly! Daddy says that we just have to wait on God to bring us a new one, but He sure is taking a long time. I'm starting to wonder if God ever wants me to get a new *Mamm*!"

"Oh, there you are!" Mandy let out a sigh of relief as she stepped into the room, "Katie, I have been looking all over the house for you! Where have you been?"

The little girl shrugged her shoulders, "Right here, Aunt Mandy!"

Mandy shook her head and took a deep breath, "*Gut* morning, Abigail. I am so sorry to keep you waiting. It's been a long time since I've had a little child around the house." Putting her hand on Katie's head, Mandy went on to say, "She's my great-niece. Katie and her dad just moved to the community and he's working to build a house. I've agreed to let them stay here and watch her during the day until his house gets finished..." Mandy took a deep breath and let it out, "I'm really not sure what he will do with her after that."

Abigail had always respected Mandy but hearing her talk of Katie as if she was nothing more than a burden broke her heart.

Katie got down on the floor to chase after a glass marble as Mandy went on to announce, "His wife died when Katie was born. If he had any sense, he would have remarried then. As things are now, he has no one to watch Katie and no hopes of things ever getting better!"

Abigail watched the little girl and shook her head sadly. It was strange to think that she wasn't the only one whose heart had been broken by loss. She knew what it was like to love someone and then lose them.

"Do you want me to get started on sewing one of these dresses?" Abigail asked softly as she motioned toward the pile of clothes.

Mandy shook her head, "Actually, I have a better use for you today, Abigail. I'll do most of the sewing if you'll just keep up with Katie. Would you mind?"

Would she mind? Abigail could think of no better job in the world!

Chapter Four

Often, Abigail found working at Mandy's to be a bit of a drag. The piles of clothing seemed never-ending and the hours would pass so slowly. Today, however, things were different.

Keeping up with Katie was the most enjoyable job that Abigail had ever done. She played hide-n-go-seek with the little girl, they baked cookies together, and they went out to the barn to look at the calves.

As the hours of the afternoon started to fade away, Abigail took Katie inside and helped her sew a little pincushion from some leftover scraps of material.

"You are a wonder with that child," Mandy announced with a smile as she watch Katie sitting quietly on the floor playing with the pincushion she had just made, "I thought I would pull my hair out before you came today!"

"She's a treasure," Abigail replied.

She was going to say more, but suddenly the voice of men interrupted her thoughts. Mandy's husband had returned home and with him was someone else.

"Aunt Mandy, where are you?"

"Back here!"

"It's Daddy!" Katie announced as she jumped up from her place on the floor, "Daddy, Daddy, come here!"

The figure of a tall man stepped into the sewing room and Katie went running to his side, "Daddy, Daddy, pick me up! I've got something to show you!"

Noah Abrams.

Abigail knew it was him as soon as she heard his voice. Although she had only seen him for a few minutes at church, it seemed she had memorized him instantly.

"Ah, a pincushion," he was exclaiming as he looked over Katie's project, "You'll have to be careful when playing with pins!"

"That's what Abigail already told me," Katie laughed as her father tickled her chin, "She's the nice lady who helped me!"

Noah finally looked up and let his eyes meet Abigail's. With a smile of recognition, he nodded his head, "Abigail Schroder, right?"

Abigail found herself tempted to look down at the floor in sudden awkwardness, "That's right."

"Abigail saved me today, Noah," Mandy was quick to announce as she cut a piece of thread on a pair of pants and put them aside, "I was able to get so much more work done while she kept Katie entertained."

"Abigail is so much fun!" Katie said with a smile before turning to Abigail, "Abigail are you going to come back to play with me tomorrow?"

"No, I'm afraid not." Abigail almost hated to tell the little girl, "I only come help your Aunt Mandy on Mondays and Fridays."

Katie's little smile quickly turned into a frown, "But I want you to come back!"

"Katie," Noah scolded gently, "Don't be rude. Miss Abigail may have other things she needs to do. You'll see her soon. Now tell her good night and go get washed up for supper."

Katie tried to smile, but her chin quivered as she got out of her father's arms and went over to give Abigail a hug.

"Bye, Abigail," the little girl whispered, "I hope you'll come back to see me again."

Mandy led Katie out of the room to go get ready for supper, leaving Noah and Abigail alone.

They stood alone in awkward silence until Abigail finally started to gather her things.

"Well," Abigail took a deep breath, "Until Friday, I suppose."

"I didn't see a buggy when I pulled up." Noah said before Abigail could reach the door, "Do you have a driver coming?"

Abigail shook her head, "I walk home."

"Don't do that. My buggy is still hitched up. I can give you a ride back while I wait on Aunt Mandy to get supper."

Abigail wanted to protest but Noah stopped her.

"No 'buts,'" he announced with a smile, "I should do something to repay you for your kindness to my little girl."

With a nod, Abigail found herself agreeing and allowed Noah Abrams to lead her out to his buggy.

Chapter Five

Abigail had not been alone with a man since Jacob left. Even though her house was just down the road, she wondered if she could bear the trip.

"I'm glad we could get a chance to talk," Noah announced as he guided his horse down the gravel drive that led to the road, "Truth be told, I'm at my wits end now that I'm here at my aunt's house. Until I get my own home finished, I have to leave Katie there and Aunt Mandy simply doesn't have the energy needed to take care of a little girl."

Abigail nodded sympathetically, "What do you plan to do?"

"Oh, things will be fine once I get my house finished and my farm up and running. I'm used to taking care of Katie. I just can't build a house with her by my side. A worksite isn't a safe place for a five-year-old."

Although Katie was a sweet child, Abigail tried to imagine how hard it would be for this poor man to try to care for her while running a farm.

"I honestly don't see how you do it all alone," Abigail announced before she could think better of her words, "It must be difficult with no wife."

Suddenly, Abigail felt her face growing warm. She wondered if her embarrassment was showing. Surely her ears must be as red as the beets that grew in her mom's garden.

"It is very rough," Noah replied with a sigh, "Even after all these years, it isn't always easy. Sometimes I doubt my ability to raise a little girl on my own but it seems to be the job that God has given me."

Abigail braved a glance at the man beside her. He looked so solemn, so completely resigned to his future. Abigail could tell that Noah Abrams had faced many difficulties in his life.

"Miss Schroder," Noah began, his voice sounding almost nervous, "I know you're too busy to even consider it, but, until I get my house finished, I need a babysitter for Katie. My aunt just can't seem to do it anymore. Would you be willing to take on the job?"

Would she?! Abigail had to fight to keep from clapping her hands in excitement. The idea of going a whole week without seeing Katie had made life seem so hollow; his job offer truly seemed like an answer to her prayers.

"Yes," She replied without any hesitation, "I can't think of anything I would love any more!"

Noah looked to Abigail and smiled. In that instant, it seemed that a weight had been lifted off his shoulders. Suddenly, he seemed carefree and happy, and whistled the rest of the way to the Schroder house.

Noah started picking Abigail up in his buggy every morning and taking her to his aunt's house where she would spend the day watching little Katie. Each day that passed, the small child became even more dear to Abigail and, surprisingly enough, so did Noah.

Abigail certainly wasn't allowing herself to entertain ideas about the handsome young widower, but she couldn't deny that a tiny shoot of hope was beginning to grow in her heart. Just like the tiny beans that had sprouted in the garden, Abigail was beginning to feel like her heart was thawing and that perhaps there was room for someone other than Jacob.

Chapter Six

Abigail had been watching little Katie daily for six weeks when Noah arrived at her house one bright Tuesday morning with a certain mischievous grin on his face. Unlike most mornings, he had small daughter at his side and a wicker basket loaded into the back of the wagon.

"*Gut* morning, Abigail!" Noah exclaimed as he reached out to help her up onto the seat, "Are you ready for a big adventure?"

Katie was grinning from ear-to-ear, leaving Abigail to wonder exactly what was up Noah Abram's sleeve.

"I don't know," Abigail replied with a laugh as she settled down on the other side of Katie, "I'm never very adventurous. What do you have planned?"

"You'll see," Noah promised with a wink.

To Abigail's surprise, Noah drove his buggy past Mandy's house and on down the road.

"Where are we going?" Katie asked, her confusion making it obvious that she was just as uncertain about the day as Abigail.

"Wait and see," Noah said as he wrapped an arm around his little child's shoulder.

Together, the three of them traveled down a small country road and turned onto a gravel driveway lined with blossoming apple trees.

"It's so beautiful!" Katie squealed as she reached out to try to touch one of the pink blossoms, "Where are we going, Daddy? This can't be the regular world, can it, Abigail?"

It certainly didn't feel like the regular world, even to Abigail. It felt like they were entering a magical land where dreams came true. Abigail took a deep breath, drawing in the scent of the wildflowers growing in the surrounding meadows. This felt like a place where she could finally release all the pain from her past and leave her worries behind.

"Look up there," Noah pointed ahead of them.

There at the end of the driveway, was a huge two-story white farmhouse.

"Oh, Daddy," Katie breathed softly, "Who owns this house?"

"We do, sweetheart!"

The house was beautiful, but it wasn't what held Abigail's attention. Instead, she found herself staring at Noah as he chatted with his daughter about their new home. It was the first time Abigail had seen him so happy. His dark brown eyes were glimmering and he was smiling like a little boy. Something about him was captivating.

Noah stopped the buggy beside the house and hopped down from his seat.

"This is it," He kept repeating as he led Katie and Abigail up onto the porch, "Sure, it's not quite finished yet. It will probably be another week before we can move in, but this is it! We have a home!"

"We have a home!" Katie repeated as she jumped up and down, clapping her hands together, "Did you hear that Abigail, we have a home!"

Abigail didn't even find herself shying away or correcting the little girl's mistake; the moment was simply too precious and Abigail discovered that she truly wished that this was her home as well.

They spend the day touring the large house and looking over the property. Noah had purchased two-hundred acres and explained his plans to build various barns to hold different animals along with his hopes to plant different kinds of grain.

Each moment that passed, Abigail found herself falling a little more in love with the man before her.

Certainly, Noah was not Jacob, but he was so much more. Selfless, caring, and gentle, Abigail wished that she had been able to meet Noah first.

Chapter Seven

Noah finished the afternoon off with a picnic by the side of the creek that trickled through his property. He had packed a delicious lunch of fried chicken, mashed potatoes, and strawberries.

"Daddy," Katie jumped up as soon as she had finished her last bite, "Can I go play in the water?"

Noah nodded, "Of course!"

Katie giggled with excitement as she hurried down to the bubbling water.

"Is she safe by herself?" Abigail asked, wondering if she should go along.

Noah nodded, "We can see her from here and the creek is only an inch deep."

Of course, Noah knew everything about the safety of the property. Abigail let out a sigh of relief as she leaned back on her elbows. She just wanted to sit peacefully and soak in the day. She wished that this afternoon never had to end.

"This is the prettiest place I've ever seen," Abigail commented.

Noah smiled, "I've always dreamed of living on a farm like this. Back in Ohio, I had a nice place, but it was just functional. I want Katie to grow up on a farm like this. It was what Lizzy wanted too..." Suddenly, his voice trailed off and his happy smile was totally replaced by something much more sober.

"Was Lizzy your wife?" Abigail ventured to ask, wondering if she should even tackle a subject that obviously brought him so much pain.

Noah nodded his head and started absentmindedly pulling pieces of grass out of the ground, "Lizzy and I got together when we were sixteen years old, and got married before we turned twenty. She was a good girl, Abigail. She had my whole heart in a way I never thought anyone else ever could..."

"What happened?"

Noah's gaze turned to the creek where his little girl was playing, "Katie happened. We wanted a baby so much, but it seems that Lizzy wasn't strong enough to handle a pregnancy. There were so many complications. When Katie was born, there was trouble and she had to go stay in the hospital. She only lived for one night." Noah shook his head, "I promised her so many things, Abigail. Promises that, sometimes, I'm not sure that I can keep. Sometimes I'm so scared that I'm going to fail her."

Noah reached up and brushed a tear away from his cheek. Watching his pain made Abigail's heart ache.

"Noah," she said in little more than a whisper, "I think you're doing everything right."

Noah turned to look at her. His eyes were red from fighting back his tears.

"*Ach*, Abigail," he muttered, "You know exactly how to help me."

In an unexpected turn of events, he reached out and gently cradled Abigail's face in his large hand.

"Daddy!" Katie's voice interrupted them, and Noah quickly withdrew.

"Daddy, Abigail, look!" Katie squealed as she came running toward their picnic spot, "I caught a fish!"

She held out her fist and revealed a tiny minnow that she had caught in the creek, "Can we cook him for supper?"

Noah and Abigail looked at each other and burst into laughter. Their special moment was over, but Abigail felt as if something between them had certainly changed forever.

Chapter Eight

Before taking her home, Noah stopped by Mandy's house.

"I'm going to take Katie in so she can go on and get ready for bed," he explained as he helped the little girl down from the buggy.

"I'll go in and say hello to your aunt," Abigail said as she took his hand in hers to get down from her seat.

Noah took Katie back into her bedroom to get changed for bed and Abigail started toward the sewing room.

As she neared the sewing room door, she could hear Mandy's voice, "Noah's almost done with his house," she was saying, "I'll be so glad once he moves out!"

Abigail lifted her hand to knock against the door, but stopped when she heard another voice speak up, "Have you seen the way that Abigail throws herself at your nephew?"

"*Ach,* yes," Abigail could see Mandy shaking her head sadly through a crack in the door, "I'm afraid that the poor girl is simply in for even more heartbreak. After being jilted by Jacob back in the spring, she must be so desperate!"

"So you don't think Noah has any interest in her?"

Mandy let out a disgusted laugh, "Most certainly not! He's used her as a babysitter, but he's had women help him out before. My sister said one girl in Ohio was almost certain that he would propose...as soon as he heard the rumors, he let her go."

Rachel Miller was clucking her tongue in condescending sadness.

"I wish he would, but Noah will never marry. He made a promise to his wife and that's final. I just wish he'd stop leading these poor girls to believe there is hope!" Mandy continued on, but Abigail couldn't bear to listen anymore. Instead, she turned and silently hurried out the side door, unwilling to wait for Noah to take her home.

Abigail couldn't stop the flood of tears that kept running down her cheeks. She wondered if she could even make it back to her house before she completely fell apart.

She could hear footsteps behind her, their sound only making it worse as she realized that she was being followed.

"Abigail," Noah called out as he ran up behind her, "Abigail, what's wrong?"

"Nothing!" Abigail exclaimed bitterly as she wrapped her arms across her chest, "I feel sick. I've got to get home."

With longer legs, Noah quickly overtook her.

"Abigail," he exclaimed as stood in front of her to block her way, "Can't I at least take you home? You've been crying! Why are you so upset? What has happened?"

"Nothing!" Abigail insisted as she stomped her foot against the ground, "Just let me go!"

When Noah saw that there was nothing he could do to stop her, he stepped out of the way and let Abigail pass.

How could I have been so foolish? Abigail asked herself as she marched down the road toward her house, *I should have never trusted another man! I should have never trusted God to have a plan for me!*

The next morning, Abigail stayed home from work. When Noah came to pick her up, she had her sister Sally go with him instead.

Chapter Nine

Each minute of the day had been agony. She had missed Katie, and she had missed Noah. How she had come to look forward to their time together! Abigail already found herself missing Noah much more than she had ever missed Jacob.

Abigail was out in the chicken house gathering eggs and trying not to cry when she heard a buggy pull into their yard.

Stepping out to check on who might be visiting, she was surprised to see Noah's buggy. On the seat beside him were Sally and Katie.

"Why are they home so early?" Abigail wondered to herself. She had planned to hide away inside the house when they returned, making it impossible to be faced with seeing him. Now she had no way to escape.

Noah scanned the yard as he helped both her sister and Katie down from the buggy.

"Where is Abigail?" She could hear the little girl ask.

"I don't know," Sally replied, "But you can come inside and we'll look for her. I'll also give you a piece of chocolate cake!"

Noah's eyes were scanning the property. When he turned to look her way, Abigail grabbed for the chicken house door, ready to hide wherever she could; however, she wasn't fast enough. In an instant, Noah's eyes were locked on her.

"Abigail, wait!" He exclaimed, making large strides in her direction, "We have to talk!"

"There's nothing to talk about."

Noah was now by her side.

"Abigail," Noah took a deep breath and caught her hand in his, "What's wrong? I thought that you were having a good time taking care of little Katie. Why would you want to quit now?"

"You don't understand, do you?" Abigail shook her head sadly, "I can't do it anymore, Noah! I just can't!"

"Why? If it's because of what happened on the picnic, I am truly sorry. I acted out of hast and I shouldn't have. I should never have touched you..."

Abigail shook her head. She couldn't let Noah think that she was rejecting him.

"No, no, no!" She exclaimed, closing her eyes and trying to keep the tears from pouring like rain, "It's not that at all. Oh, Noah, you don't understand. I overheard your aunt talking. She said that you will never get married again, that your wife made you promise that you wouldn't! I can't stand to lose you, Noah, I just can't! I love you far too much for that. If we can't ever be together, than I can't be around you at all!"

Noah let out something that sounded almost like a sigh of relief, "Abigail, dear Abigail," he reached up and gently brushed away her tears with the tip of his finger, "I thought that you hated me. You poor, dear girl! My aunt knows some things, but she doesn't know everything. When Lizzy died, she did make me promise things. She made me promise that I would take care of Katie, that I would love her, that I would do what was best for her, that I would give her a good home...and then she made me promise that I would not marry again until I found someone who I truly love, someone who will take good care of our little girl and who will take good care of me. Abigail, I have avoided women for that very reason. I have never felt like God had put the right one in my path. I never felt like any woman I met would ever be able to fill the void that Lizzy left in my heart."

His words...they almost gave her hope. Abigail took a deep breath and shook her head, "Noah, I know you can never feel that way about me."

Noah put his hands on her shoulders and stared into her eyes, "Abigail, you don't know how special you've become to me."

Suddenly, the words broke something deep inside of Abigail. It felt like the wall she had built around her heart was suddenly shattered into a million pieces as she realized that she truly did have hope.

"It can be hard to explain what is in my heart," Noah whispered as he leaned his forehead against hers, "But you need to know that what is in my heart is you, Abigail Schroder."

"Oh Noah," she whispered the words softly against his lips, "You are my whole heart as well."

Suddenly, their lips met in love's first kiss. As Noah pulled her closer against his strong body, Abigail could feel her broken heart begin to heal. Just when she thought that God had given up on her future, He had continued to work out His plans in her life. When Abigail had been ready to give up on ever having her own family, God had brought this wonderful *gut* man to her side.

Once their kiss was over, Abigail found herself leaning her head against this dear man's shoulder.

"Noah," she whispered gently, "Oh, Noah, I do love you so."

Suddenly, the sound of childish laughter brought them back to reality as Katie emerged from the large farmhouse and started bouncing across the yard.

"Daddy," Katie squealed as she ran to him and wrapped her arms around his legs, "Does this mean I'm going to get a new *Mamm*?"

Noah looked at Abigail and winked.

"It just might," he told her as he scooped the little girl up into his arms, "We will just have to ask her." Turning to look at Abigail, Noah asked, "Miss Schroder, would you do us the honor of being Katie's new *Mamm*? And my new wife?"

Abigail could hardly speak over the pounding of her joyful heart, "Nothing would make me any happier!"

She reached out and wrapped her arms around both Noah and Katie, pulling her new family close against her.

God truly had a plan after all.